One Day I'll Tell You the Things I've Seen

One Day I'll Tell You
the Things I've Seen

Stories

SANTIAGO VAQUERA-VÁSQUEZ

University of New Mexico Press · Albuquerque

Library of Congress Cataloging-in-Publication Data

Vaquera-Vásquez, Santiago R., 1966–
[Short stories. Selections]
One day I'll tell you the things I've seen : stories / Santiago Vaquera-Vásquez.
   pages ; cm
Some text previously published in Spanish.
ISBN 978-0-8263-5573-7 (softcover : acid-free paper) — ISBN 978-0-8263-5574-4 (electronic)
I. Title.
PS3622.A69A6 2015
813'.6—dc23
                                                        2014031880

Cover photograph: *I Couldn't Spill My Heart*, 2007, courtesy of Santiago Vaquera-Vásquez
Designed by Catherine Leonardo
Composed in ScalaOTRegular

The following stories have been previously published in different form:
"Over There on the Other Side," published in Spanish as "Migrante aún no identificado #5"
   in *72 migrantes* (72migrantes.com) and later published by the *Editorial Almadía* in 2011.
"Sleepwalker," published in Spanish as "Sonámbulo" in the online project *54 semanas*,
   organized by Erik Molgora.
"One Day I'll Tell You the Things I've Seen," published in Spanish as "Algún día te cuento las
   cosas que he visto" in my chapbook *Algún día te cuento las cosas que he visto* (2012).
"Lonely Planet," published in Spanish and English in *MAKE: A Literary Magazine*.
"Despedidas," published in Spanish as "Despedidas" in *Revista Número 0*.
"Lupe and the Stars," published in Spanish as "Lupe bajo las estrellas" in *Iowa Literaria*.
"Days without Paracetamol," published in Spanish as "Paracetamol" in *Camino Real*.
"La línea," published in Spanish as "Estampas de Califas" in *Ventana Abierta*.

Para mi madre, Dora Luz Vásquez, for her strength,
her fierceness, her stories, and her support.

Para JD, LAU, LHC, AF, EPS, DS, SR, RRHS, AE:
friends, teachers, and companions.

Para Lauren, for the story we began on that night
we drove across a stormy plain for truck-stop coffee.

As always, I carry your star, embroidered. Over
my heart—this plenum & plain universe.

—Juan Felipe Herrera

En esta noche: que me valga la memoria
para nombrar las cosas como fueron.

—Tino Villanueva

Contents

Over There on the Other Side

Who will know us when we breathe through the grass?
—Gary Soto

LA LÍNEA HAS MANY stories.

Once while waiting to cross, Moms told me about the time she and my dad first crossed la línea. It wasn't that hard. Maybe it was because it was the 1960s, decades before various border-patrol operations made it difficult to cross without papers. Maybe it was because they were from the border that no one questioned when they pulled up to the agent in their borrowed white Mustang. For the agent, they were just a pair of teenagers in love. One of those good-looking couples who crossed because they wanted to cruise around el otro lado. Maybe they were planning to take a walk around downtown Calexico. Maybe they were going shopping in El Centro. Maybe they were just going to Brawley for ice cream. And after their cruise, they would return in their ranfla to Mexicali. Maybe that's what went through the border agent's mind as he let them pass without asking too many questions. So easy. So quick.

I am waiting in a long line. There are about fifteen cars ahead of me. I look at those around me, at the drivers, at their faces. Some are tired, some bored, some anxious, and a few, just a few, are nervous. It is hot and we are all waiting in cars, waiting to cross la línea, that line that in other areas is called the border.

It is no longer so easy or so quick to cross the border.

A man passes by selling newspapers. The main story is about the seventy-two undocumented migrants massacred in northern Mexico. Many of the victims remain unidentified. I think about one of them, one of those anonymous victims massacred senselessly. One who decided to leap: leave his country, cross Mexico, and then cross into the United States. One, as so many others before, who would not make it. One who would remain in the registries as a number: Unidentified Migrant #5.

Between the lines of cars, I see people selling candy and water, Red Cross volunteers asking for donations, kids carrying rags and large bottles of water to clean windshields. I see a man without legs pushing himself in a wheelchair, a tin cup on his lap. I see a long wait in a long line.

My father died the same day the Unidentified Migrant #5 was murdered in Tamaulipas, was massacred alongside seventy-one others who he might or might not have known. I think of the people who arrived for my father's burial. People who came to say good-bye under a blue sky and the August Mexicali heat. People, some like my father, who crossed the border illegally in search of a better life. Some stayed, others came back, and a few went missing.

Unidentified Migrant #5, the one who left his country to cross to the other side: the one who accepted the weight of being undocumented so that he could earn money for his family. Maybe he was convinced by an enganchador who promised him loads of dollars and more over there in El Norte. Maybe he left because he had a young wife who was pregnant. Maybe he had a relative over there, someone who could help him get a good job to pay back the enganchador. Of course he must have heard about the danger: the possibility of being robbed or kidnapped, or the likelihood of being enslaved by some cartel. If he did have family on the other side, there was always the chance of losing a finger, a hand, an arm, if he was unable to come up with the ransom. Of course the danger would have seemed small before the promise of the good life that awaited him over there in El Norte. Allá en el otro lado.

Over there on the other side: that limit that in other parts is called border.

Unidentified migrant #5 will never know the other side.

He will never add his story to la línea as my parents did. He will never know the long lines waiting to cross. He will never pass through the fields of cotton of Texas; the strawberry fields, the orange groves, the olive orchards of California; the meat-packing plants of the Midwest; the construction sites of Chicago and New York City. He will never feel the winter chill of the Northeast, nor the damp summer heat of the South. He will remain just a statistic in the sad history of migration and become just a memory in his family's history: the uncle, the brother, the father who left for the other side and never came back. He will remain like my father, a blurry memory of a figure saying good-bye from a doorway and driving away in his car.

My turn. The border guard scrutinizes me from behind dark sunglasses. In his hand he holds my passport. He checks out the old white Mustang that I'm driving.

What are you bringing from Mexico? he asks.

Nothing. Nothing more than my dead, I want to respond.

But I simply say: Nothing.

Sleepwalker

MONTHS LATER, THE SAME nightmare: I had fallen into the irrigation ditch and the current was taking me to the tunnel beneath the highway. I would flail in my sleep in an attempt to get out of the ditch and onto the ground.

My brother Todd suffered this same dark dream. There were nights when I would awake to hear him thrashing in his bed, raising his arms, diving under the covers, grabbing a pillow, and then breathing deeply, knowing that he had saved me.

Todd was a sleepwalker. He acted out his dreams with such intensity that Moms had to lock the bedroom door at night so he wouldn't get away. For years, I lived these dreams too: we shared a room. He would kick the air. Applaud. Act out scenes from *Star Wars*. Shit like that. One night, Moms forgot to lock the door and he walked out. I followed. We walked down the quiet street by the light of the moon. I watched the homes of my mostly sleeping neighbors. There were a few televisions on, occasionally a dim light, but mainly the houses were dark. At Daniel's house I saw a shadow in the window. My tía, I thought. Waiting as she always did. We wandered around the hood until I could finally guide my brother back home. After that night, he had to go to bed zipped up in a sleeping bag to restrict his movements.

His voice on the phone: barely audible. Hoarse. There's a lot of noise on the line, ruido blanco. He calls from beyond a storm of static: a voice calling from another planet. As a kid he was a sleep-walker. Now he is an insomniac. I can see him standing there, whispering to me on the phone. He's too thin; his gaze, distant and blank. I know that he is nervously scratching at the scars that mark his arms. He's telling me about his trip to Soledad. I look out the window. Snow. His voice coming from across three thousand miles of continent and three time zones: he in San Francisco, I in Hanover, New Hampshire.

A storm of ruido blanco between us, his voice scrambled in the nightworld.

There is a photo of us together taped to the wall of my dorm room. We are standing on a hill. Behind us are the ditch and the orchard. He is dressed in that style he brought back with him after his first year at Cornell: khaki pants, ironed flannel shirt buttoned to the top, shiny calcos. No one could understand why he returned with that moda, that very East Los look. An urban SoCal cholo look showing up in rural Northern Califas. Me, I am in my usual uniform of jeans, black T-shirt with the Green Lantern logo, and scuffed Nike shoes.

He went to Soledad because they said he'd find our father there. I never understood why he insisted on looking for that cabrón. Maybe he thought he could save him. Todd had always been that way, looking for damaged people to save. Maybe he thought he could save himself in the process.

One morning, Todd walked out of the camper where he was

crashing and headed for the nearby hills. The insomnia made everything more intense: the colors, the sky, the landscape. A stop sign captivated him. Dark stains appeared to be eating the white S-T-O-P. The letters slowly dripped down into the red and mixed with the stains. They meant something dark and horrible.

Freaky, ése. I touched that sign and felt an odd vibra. Neta, bróder. I felt like those manchas sensed me and began to move toward my fingers. I lifted my hand and, I don't know . . . I felt something strange. A heavy sense of cansancio. I fell asleep right there.

He says all this and then sighs.

He dreamed. He was sitting beneath the stop sign when Dad drove up in a black car. Todd stood up and called to him. No response. The car moved forward, heading toward the hills. Todd began to chase the car, yelling out his name. He couldn't catch up. He slipped and fell beside the road.

I woke up when I hit a rock. I stood up. I was alone in the hills. Scratched up. Bleeding from one of my knees.

And?

And nothing. Nada. I walked down the hill to the camper. Never found our dad. I always arrive five minutes after he leaves. The only thing I find is his echo.

A long silence. I hear someone ask my brother something. No response. Then I hear him sighing deeply.

I saved you, bróder. Do you remember? That time you fell into the acequia?

Of course. Maybe tal vez I'll save you sometime, I said.

Doubt it, ése. Doubt it a lot. Check this, bróder. Check out what I'm going to tell you. Ready? Tell Moms that I know how this will end.

What?

Ruido blanco on the line. Coughing. The hoarse, whispered voice that comes from a long ways away.

I know how this will end.

And then silence.

I am left holding the phone. Wind. Static.

I close my eyes and see the stop sign. The melting letters. The dark stains. The echo of a person who could no longer be saved.

She Would Tell Stories

MY MOTHER, OLDER BUT still looking young, lights a candle every morning at the altar for my sister, then runs a hand over the ceramic urn that holds the ashes.

She'll then sit at her chair and close her eyes.

When we were children I remember her telling stories while standing at the window. Outside the fall rain would descend in large drops that would splash on the ground. She would tell stories while looking out at the drowning yard. She watched rivers of recently seeded lawn loosening and spreading over the sidewalk. She watched as her carefully tended rose garden turned into a mud pit. Her black hair covering part of her face; her eyes weary after a long day at the nut-packing plant; her mouth tired after hours of yelling over machinery. She would look outside, telling stories while she waited: for her children to fall asleep; for her husband to come home. The lights of the white Mustang cutting through the rain and illuminating the new house.

She was young. Too young to be a mother. Too young to have followed her husband to a small town a thousand miles north of the border and far from her home. Too young to live in that agricultural town when she had grown up in a large border city where every weekend she could go out dancing, go out to the movies, or just go out for a walk on the busy downtown streets.

Young. Too young.

And we would watch her, my sister and I, while she told us stories. She would tell us about her border town, about the dances and the Friday-night parties, the cruises along the boulevard in her cousin's car on Saturday nights, the trips to the movies on Sunday afternoons. She was considered one of the prettiest women in her barrio, and there were always guys from other areas trying to catch her eye. Instead, these dudes usually met the fists of some batos from the hood who were not about to let some interlopers from another colonia scoop up their women. Usually, the fists were attached to her oldest brother, who was considered el Rey del Barrio. He was the best looking, the best dancer, and the best fighter. He was known in all the surrounding barrios and he was respected.

But my father didn't know el Rey. He saw my mother one afternoon when she was working at the record store and he realized that he wanted to be by her side. My moms turned and saw my jefe looking at her. And then she saw him walk into a tree. And in that moment, Moms also wanted to be by his side.

My jefe drove into the barrio the following weekend with his brother. It didn't take him long to find out where Moms lived. He was at the wheel of a borrowed white Mustang. He sent his younger brother to knock at my abuelo's door. The batos from the hood stood around, waiting for my uncle to put a stop to yet another pretendiente to my mother. For some reason, the beating didn't happen. My moms intervened.

The batos from the hood were not impressed. Later, when my

jefe made another trip into the barrio, they jumped him. It was my uncle who stepped in. He then laid down the law: my father was off-limits. He was allowed to walk the streets of the barrio, and anyone who disagreed would have to answer to my tío and his fists.

And that was that.

And she would stand at the window, looking out at her flooded lawn, and tell us stories. Stories about over there, far, far from here. Here where she didn't have cousins to hang out with or an older brother who would protect her.

And we would listen to her stories while she waited for the lights of my father's car to pull into the driveway of our new house, recently built, recently bought. It was the beginning of the American Dream. This was the house she had dreamed of for many years, with a big front yard where she would plant her roses and a large backyard where Dad would lay a cement patio and plant fruit trees. This was the house where she was finally going to be able to put down roots.

Here was where she was going to have her family united. Everything was going to be wonderful. She would never have to wait long nights for an arrival. Together she and her husband would build on her American Dream.

Here. Here was where there would be no drunken arguments, no beatings on the nights when he would drink away his paycheck and come home staggering with blazing eyes.

Here. Here was going to be where things would work out and there would no longer be summers in northern Mexico where we would listen to her beg our abuelo to let her come home.

Here, here, in the new house with a husband who would arrive to spend the night by her side and not by someone he met in the bar.

And she would wait. And wait. And wait.

She would tell us stories, and we listened to her talk as a way to forget her geography of pain, her trail of scars leading from here to her home over there. And in her stories she would have a shiny new house, with a united family and beautiful flowers growing in the garden.

And everything.

Everything.

Everything would be in its right place.

Homeboys

MY COUSIN LALO. As kids we all called him Eddie. But in high school, he became Lalo. Homeboy had an older brother, Todd. Todd was the first child in his family to be born on this side de la línea. And as the shit was heavy for Mexicanos in those days, his jefes decided to give him a problem-free name. A gringo name. Todd. But he was screwed when it came to his last name. Rodríguez. No way to hide that nopal nailed to his forehead. Todd Rodríguez. A messed up bróder, bifurcated in name. Eso sí, he was the star child of that familia. He was the older brother who was going to save his family from la misería after the divorce of his folks that hit his family with the force of a hydrogen bomb. A lot of people in town also suffered collateral damage. Smart bato, though. Made it to the top of his class in high school. Sure, it was a rural high school in Northern Califas. Orland, a tiny speck of town lost in the orange groves and the olive orchards. But still. It was enough for some recruiter from the East

Coast—I don't know, maybe he took a left at Sacramento when he should have taken a right—to offer him a scholarship to Cornell.

It would have all been un final feliz, the typical happy ending—farmer boy makes good, let's quickly put up the words The End on the screen and get the audience out of here—if that dumbass Todd had not died a junkie in some callejón in San Francisco.

That was some messed up shit.

Homeboy could not hang with the white elite of Cornell who had brought out a child of migrant workers in one of those liberal acts of kindness to deposit him in a whole other class structure. Shit blew his mind. Rise in social class that rapidly without preparation? C'mon. That's beyond science fiction. One could end up with a deep case of the bends. Resulted that Todd was out of place: unable to hang with either those richie riches or with the rich, urban Hispanics from the affluent Latino suburbs who saw him like some alien brought from another planet. Despite his American name. And instead of assimilating into the country-club set, homes became a stereotype. He dressed in that 'chuco style from cities like Stockton or Sacras. And worse, the loser became an addict, strung out on las drugs del momento. He failed out of Cornell. The university was unprepared to deal with a bato like him. He finished homeless y wasted on the streets of San Francisco. He became just another statistic and excuse for tapado conservatives to declare that Affirmative Action was a fracaso.

Todd, he was familia, but he wasn't really a cuate of mine.

My homeboy was Lalo, Todd's younger brother who was around my age. We were tight as kids. This primo was able to leave the pueblo, make it into Dartmouth, and actually survive in a town even more lost than Ithaca. All this despite the fears of his moms that he would end up a cartoon gangster like his older brother. One time, Lalo told me about these few Hispanics from Southern California. Self-hate leaked from their skin. They were the ones who came from money but denied it, as if being upper-middle class were a disease. They wanted to be farmworkers and claimed to be authentically attached to the land so they could say that they knew discrimination. But deep down they knew that when things got tough, they could run to Papi and his money. Born with silver spoons, they wanted to eat off of paper plates. At first, they expected Lalo to confirm their condition of suffering Hispanics, but the bato was a punk rocker. Unlike me, the dude could play an instrument, whereas I was just a DJ at a punk rock radio station. Anyway, homes played bass in a band. He taught his band how to play "La Bamba," the punk version by the Plugz. The one that ended with the lead singer screaming that he wasn't a capitalist, but an anarchist. Homeboy survived those white winters and then bounced around different countries while doing graduate work in New York and San Diego. Now the bato teaches at the University of Iowa.

Lalo asked me if I remembered el freak del Xipe. Juan Nepucemio Nepucemio, alias el Xipe. His pops had been a masked luchador in Mexico City. His name, I think, was Doctor Avalancha: Temblor del Cielo. But things had been tough for him, too many masked luchadores in that big city. I think it was because his name was too long. Mi jefe saw him wrestle a couple of times back then. The announcers were always changing his name. Doctor Avalancha: Temblor del Cielo was too much. They just called him Terremoto. That would really piss him off. His mask was black with what looked like a white tree rising on the front.

And since he couldn't make it in Mexico, he ended up in los Estados Unidos working first as a bracero in los files. Later, he was able to pick up work in a carpa that traveled around the Southwest. They were looking for wrestlers. And since he still had his mask, the old man ran off to join the circo. I saw him once when the carpa came to town. He was going under the name El Vengador Azteca. It wasn't his idea. The announcers knew that the majority of their public was Mexican, and so they figured with this new name he'd get a truckload of fans. And that's how it was. The bato was very popular among la raza who worked long hours in the field, in the packing companies, or as mechanics and gardeners.

Here he comes! ¡Ai viene! ¡El vengador! And he would step out onto the stage to the tune of "El jinete" by José Alfredo. Some of the announcers could never pronounce his name right and they would yell out "the Beinguhdorrr Azzzzsshteicahhhh!"

But in the end, Doctor Avalancha: Temblor del Cielo left. He left like a lot of pops do. Seeking out new luchas and other stages. His kid Xipe kept the mask. And sometimes, that freak would cruise around town wearing it. He would stop in front of the reflective window of the JCPenney and make wrestling poses. He would head over in the mask to the Saturday matinees at the cine. He would wander around the aisles of Big John's Supermarket, a masked kid carrying a comic book. He was smart, too. But he was just another bright kid with too many possibilities who opted for nothing. And then he disappeared. No one knows where.

One Day I'll Tell You
the Things I've Seen

SOMETIMES WHEN I'M OUT there, I suddenly rea
know where I am. And then I have to sit down and r
places I've been. Monday: breakfast with friends in Sa
That night, I had an early dinner with different friends
tan. Tuesday: Paris. With my terrible, horrible, minim
even though I had been to Paris five times in the last si
made my way to my favorite hotel where they alrea
well. Thursday: traveled by Eurostar to London fo:
meeting in the City. That evening I flew to Amsterda
at Zoo Station in Berlin I waited around for some fr:
few months ago in Tokyo. Sunday: rest in Barcelona
ing: coffee in the KLM Crown Lounge at Schipol air|
my way to California before hopping on another flig

Andrea tells all of this to Daniel. They've met, a
years, in Newark. Daniel doesn't like to travel much
he had accepted a university position where he was a

so. He was told that he would spend at least four months of the year outside of the country. Daniel was sitting at a bar trying to forget about his upcoming flight when Andrea sat down beside him.

When he saw her he thought of something Bogart never said: Of all the broken-down airport gin joints, in all the towns, in all the world, she walks into mine. He realized then that his life was made up of those strips of film that are edited out of the final movie and dumped, forgotten, into the trash.

And you know, because of all this travel I've gotten used to airports, Andrea confesses. Even though I've traveled pretty much all over the world in the past year, I don't think I could really tell you a lot about the places I've been. More than anything, I know their airports. And I've come to realize that I keep running into the same people: everyone en route to somewhere. Everyone with sensible luggage that contains their lives and can be stored in an overhead bin. Everyone on a never-ending trip, passing through airports that after a while all start to look the same until the world becomes a giant airport where cities and towns are nothing more than boarding lounges.

Daniel. He has no idea how to respond.

When he was twenty years old, he felt uncertain about everything, he had difficulties talking to anyone, and when it came to meeting girls, he would freeze up and start to feel faint. Homeboy was wicked shy. When not in the painting studio, Daniel was often hiding out at the campus radio station where he had a music program. His program ran from 10 p.m. to 2 a.m. on Saturday nights. When most players were out on the streets, Daniel was in a music studio, spinning records and building the soundtrack for those of us who were out.

He preferred it that way, locked in the studio spinning vinyl records and putting on his favorite songs: Cure, "A Forest"; X-Mal Deutschland, "Mondlicht"; Wire Train, "Love Against Me." It was in the studio that the compa found his voice; surrounded by records he could construct his own personal soundtrack to his life. He had

complete freedom to play whatever he wanted. He mixed genres, time periods, and would play fast songs followed by slow songs followed by whatever weird dirge thing he could dig out of the archives. There would be Elvis Presley followed by Elvis Costello. "96 Tears" by ? and the Mysterians paired with "Don't Give It Up Now" by Lyres. "I'm Straight" by the Modern Lovers with "Venus in Furs" by the Velvet Underground. Or he would have a set of music that would include the Clash, followed by a norteño song like "Eslabón con eslabón" by Los Invasores de Nuevo León, which would then be followed by something from the Specials and then Los Lobos. Or he would do a set of straight-up punk with Sex Pistols, the Ramones, the Dead Kennedys, and suddenly there would be "I'm Not in Love" by 10cc followed by Lords of the New Church with "Live for Today." It made for some crazy playlists, but those of us who tuned in could not help but feel impressed at the dude's mixes. I was tripping for days with a pairing he did of Malcolm McLaren's "Buffalo Gals" with Enrico Caruso doing "Vesti la giubba."

I met the homeboy in an anthropology class that we both signed up for because of the title, "Magic, Witchcraft, and Religion." It was taught in this large theater over in the art building. The professor would often step out from behind this curtain and start lecturing, pacing the stage and talking about religious practices around the world. I kept hoping he would one day appear dressed up as Doctor Strange or Mandrake the Magician. After the first couple of weeks, I thought of switching from my geography major to anthropology. The class was that fucking cool.

Daniel often sat near me in the back of the auditorium. He would always come in with headphones clamped onto his head— they were the only things that kept his crazy hair under control. His eyes were often bloodshot. Too many bong hits, I originally thought. Fucking tecato. Especially with that weird mumbly sort of high-pitched voice of his. But I later found out that the bato never partook of drugs and rarely drank alcohol. At least, not until la

Diabla came into his life. The night we drove south he got into this weird confessional mood as we passed the rice fields and he said it was all on account of an abusive alcoholic father who abandoned his family when he was thirteen. This tragedy was later followed by the cancer of his sister and the months he spent by her side in the cancer ward. So, while most young machos in training were experimenting with drink and drugs and chicas, homeboy was watching his sister die. Now, it tears me up when I think about it, but back then I was not that sympathetic. I knew the tragedy of being marooned on Cancer Island too, and I also knew about abandonment by a father. And though I didn't want to get into it, I thought the coincidences between our lives were fucking weird, and the fact that we shared the same name was crazy. I told D as we were crossing the bridge over the river that he should snap out of it, he needed to man up, that he was just looking for excuses. Homeboy just stared at me like the fucking monster that I was.

We didn't talk for another two hours, until we had passed Sacramento.

I didn't care. I just kept thinking the whole situation was too busted.

He wore shirts found at the Goodwill and fatigue pants bought at the army supply store. The fatigues were often paint-stained, as he would sometimes clean his brushes on them. He also almost always wore these huaraches made in Mexico, the ones with the rubber-tire soles. He often slunk down in the back of the class, and I thought he wasn't paying attention, but after the first midterm I realized that the bato was bordering on some genius-level shit.

He just pretended to be an idiot.

I later realized he wasn't pretending there either. The bato had a serious lack of self-confidence. He was convinced that no one ever remembered who he was. I once saw him completely stop talking to someone he used to occasionally chat with because he assumed that she didn't remember him. It was fucking weird. He believed that he passed through the world without leaving a mark.

I tried to work with the bato, but it was no use. Homeboy was riven with insecurities. The one who sort of got him out of his shell, out of his youthful stupor? A fellow DJ at the radio station: L.A. Betty. Her real name was María, but she wanted something cooler, more punk, for her radio name. The original AlternaTina from East L.A., she headed north from her home base of Los Angeles to study radio production in our small university town in NorCal. She's the one who gave the bato his first radio name: Farmer Dan. The first time he met her, she introduced herself as Los Angeles Betty, L.A. Betty, La Bet-T. She marched into the studio carrying her favorite record, *Attitudes* by the Brat, and declared: Teresa Covarrubias is it. Respect her. And to demonstrate, she moved behind the console, took off the record he had cued up, and pulled the disc out of its sleeve. Holding it aloft, she dramatically placed it on the turntable, turned to Daniel, blew him a kiss, cut off the song he was playing—Depeche Mode's "Photographic"—and started up "Leave Me Alone."

How could he not let someone like that open him right up?

Bet-T's radio show was on after his, on the 2–6 a.m. slot. Sometimes, he would stay in the studio for her whole show and the two would wander out into the streets at six in the morning and head to Jake's Diner for coffee before going to her place where they would collapse on her bed.

Betty would often get mad because he never suggested going to his place.

He didn't because he thought that would imply a committed relationship and neither of them ever thought of themselves as anything even approximating boyfriend-girlfriend. Rather, she described Daniel as her lover, while he considered himself nothing more than a passing fancy in her life. There were nights she would arrive early to catch the end of his radio program and to do whatever she could to break his concentration. One time she bit on his ear while he was reading a station ID, another time she unbuttoned his pants. At first these kinds of things annoyed him, but later he came to the conclusion that it didn't matter what went on over the air since he didn't believe that anyone would waste their Saturday nights listening to his radio program.

But of course he had listeners. There was me, for instance. And I was more of an avid listener in those months when I was hiding out because I had made the mistake of going out with not one, not two, not three, but four chicas in the same small college town. Once they found out they started roaming the bars and clubs together, and so I had to stop going out in case they caught me. Again.

So. Saturday nights were indoors listening to D on the radio. Sometimes I would kick it with him in the studio, but I always got a weird vibe off Bet-T. She threw me some serious shade. I called her la Diabla. She was not down with me in general, and she hated when I was at the studio ruining whatever freak show she had planned for the two of them. One night, when I was over there chilling with a Tecate, she threatened to call Las Four and tell them where I was hiding. Cabrona.

Daniel's most avid listener was probably Andrea. She was nuts about his program and his mixes. One time, she told him that he must have some direct connection to her brain because he always knew what song to play. She would dance to the Cure in her basement apartment, sing along with Gang of Four, and she would always be blown away when all of a sudden D would play some old Chicano barrio rola from someone like Malo or El Chicano. Rolas that often didn't fit with the punk rock format of the station but somehow still made sense.

So there he is, sitting at the bar drinking a beer with the hopes that it will calm his nerves when he hears his name. He looks up and doesn't recognize her at first. And then the VCR that is his memory lurches on and starts the movie where she and he are the protagonists.

There she is.

Andrea.

Twenty years later.

Andrea was born in Redwood City. Her pops was a therapist in San Francisco; her moms, a doctor. They were ex-hippies who became yuppies.

Huppies, Andrea once said, because they were Hispanic. She spat the word out with difficulty. At one point, she once told him, they were Chicano. They were in the movimiento y todo. But now. Now they're *Hiss*spanics. She was uncomfortable with the word, thinking that it meant giving up on social activism. Even still, it was obvious that Andrea basked in the class privilege that her parents gave her. One time, Daniel commented that it was clear that she had never had to suffer for anything in life.

It was an error. Bad thing to say, dude, I told him as we sat at a bar.

She didn't talk to him for a week.

He left her in the most idiotic, pendejo way you could imagine. It was his last radio show at the end of the semester, the night before graduation. He had no plans to go to the ceremony. His idea was to leave town right after his show and head south. His stuff had already been moved to his mom's and my car was packed with what he needed for the summer. We were driving south together. I would take him as far as Tijuana and he would then hop on a flight to Mexico City, and from there he was thinking of taking a bus to Oaxaca.

He had not seen Andrea in a week because they were both busy with finals. Aside from his family and me, no one else knew about his escape plan. I went with him for his final program, and before he turned on the mic, he said, This whole show is for you, Andrea. At the end of his program he signed off: One day I'll tell you the things I've seen.

Fucking dramatic if you ask me.

His whole plan to bounce was typical of his weirdness. If it hadn't been for the fact that I had a car, the bato would have cut me off like he did everyone else. He figured that it didn't matter if he left like that, especially since he believed that once gone he would be instantly forgotten, erased from the VCR, deleted from the memory banks.

La Diabla was busy with her family that night, so she had some other DJ cover for her. While that dude was pulling out records for his first set, Daniel packed his record bag quickly and quietly. He said a few words to the DJ, hefted his bag over his shoulder, and then we were out into the warm night. We hopped in my car, pulled out of the parking lot, and headed out of town. I asked D if he wanted to do a short loop around downtown, but he said he wanted to get on the road. Soon we were driving with the windows down through the almond orchards and the rice fields before crossing the river and getting on the interstate that would take us south.

Daniel was gone for four years. He landed a gig teaching English in Oaxaca. Sometimes he would send me letters that I would receive at my university address. I would read them on the beach before having to go back to sit in on my graduate seminars. Those letters got me through part of grad school.

He would drink beer with tourists he met in the zócalo. One time he ran into la Diabla. He was sitting in a bar listening to norteño music on the jukebox when she strolled in with some friends. They both stared at each other in surprise. Two hours later, they were in her hotel room, lying on her bed with the street sounds coming in from outside the open window. A few days after that, the two took a bus to the coast where they spent their time lying on the beach, dancing, and drinking in cheap bars until late, and then sleeping until the afternoon. Before returning home, he took her to his apartment. Getting dressed in the morning she looked at him and said, It's about time you forgot about her.

Andrea.

It had been four years.

He could barely remember what she looked like.

La Diabla hated her. To her, Andrea was nothing more than a

chava who, since she couldn't be white, opted to be an exotic Latina. She couldn't stand the way she dressed: indigenous huipiles, rebozos, large silver earrings. Betty had her dark hair dyed black black, she had pale skin, raccoon-painted eyes, and her lips were often coated a bright, bloody red. She moved to the soundtrack of X, los Illegals, the Brat, the Plugz, and the Zeros. She wore black jeans, punk band T-shirts, and heavy, black boots. A punk Chicana: L.A. Betty.

Betty was convinced that any interest that Andrea had in the plight of the poor was nothing more than show. The moment that cabrona starts to feel suffering—she would tell Daniel and me with her eyes narrowed—she is going to run to Papi to save her ass.

Daniel never said anything, even though he also knew that Betty would never really know suffering since she also came from privileged roots.

And now there she is again, Andrea. She is working for a global telecommunications company. Her job meant that she had to travel all over the world. My abuelito was a bracero in California. He worked picking olives, grapes, and strawberries. Now look at me, I'm a cyber bracera. Instead of strawberries in Oxnard, I'm working fiber-optic cables in London. Instead of grapes in Fresno, I'm working mobile networks in Tokyo. Instead of olives in Orland, I have the telecommunication centers in Helsinki. I don't have a central office; any space where I can plug in is my workspace. I once had a meeting with team members in Manhattan, Hong Kong, and London while I was traveling on Thalys from Brussels to Paris.

Andrea. She had not changed. She was always moving at light speed. With the energy that she released, she could light up Manhattan for at least a decade.

Daniel stares at her, not knowing how to respond.

She tells him that she is stopping in San Francisco on her way to Tokyo, then on to Hong Kong. She had to stop in Newark because she had to check in with some people in Manhattan. Daniel tells her that he's on his way to Mexico City. A new job.

I don't like to fly. It makes me nervous, he confesses, reaching for his beer.

Don't think about the trip. Think more on the point of arrival, she tells him.

Is that what you do?

Andrea looks out the window at the jets parked at the gates. No, she responds. The truth is I don't know where that is. I only have the trip.

Daniel wants to tell her something. But the beer and the emotions of seeing her again keep him from forming coherent thoughts.

She called him only once in those years when he was a DJ. She wanted to request a song. Actually, it was her boyfriend who made the request. "Our Lips Are Sealed" by the Go-Go's. An obvious choice. After playing it, he followed with the version by the Fun Boy Three. He ended that set of music with "Love Will Tear Us Apart." Near the end of his show la Diabla entered the station with a troop of skaters, punks, and painters. She had started a party at her house, but then decided to bring everyone over. Even though she asked, he didn't feel like hanging around. Before stepping outside, Betty pulled him aside and told him that she wanted a private meeting with him in the main office. Maybe tal vez later, he responded, and left.

Daniel ended up at Jake's at two in the morning to have some coffee. He didn't expect to see anyone and walked into the diner with his record bag and a large sketchbook to work on a project. He ran into Andrea and her boyfriend from out of town, some dude named Lloyd. When she saw Daniel her face lit up while he tried to contain his own emotions. Lloyd checked him out and then said that while he liked the show, he thought Daniel talked too much between sets. Less talk, more rock, the pendejo recommended. Daniel didn't respond, but he could tell that Andrea was pissed at the remark. Daniel walked to the counter, ordered a coffee to go, and headed out.

That was the last time he saw Lloyd. Upon leaving Jake's, Andrea dumped his ass on the street.

She had a basement apartment close to downtown. In her room, she had posters of the Cure, the Smiths, and R.E.M. Sometimes after class, she and Daniel would grab a coffee and head to her place. Occasionally, she would put on music and ask him to dance: together they would bounce around her living room in that herky-jerky '80s style. Those nights after leaving her place, he would ride his bike to his apartment in a strange euphoria. He would sit in his living room. He wouldn't turn on the radio or the TV. Just silence. He would sit there in the dark and think about his moments with Andrea. He would think about her long, dark-brown hair, her café con leche skin, her laugh as they would dance around.

He knew he couldn't live like that. Not with that feeling inside.

The truth is they were never more than friends, despite there being some strong connection between them.

And it's not like the bato had no game. The boy had G, but he didn't realize it. I don't know, maybe he was fucked up by his home-life. But something happened there. A bomb went off in his past with the blast continuing into his present. Something. Something with the power of a Godzilla-level Oxygen Destroyer: a G destroyer. Dude believed he left no wake. Or maybe it was like that episode of the X-Files where the guy is afraid of his own shadow, afraid because his shadow is in actuality a black hole. In D's case maybe that black hole was a fucked up curse that threatened to swallow him whole. That night as we drove south, somewhere outside of Los Angeles, he told me his brain was full of old locked boxes and he wasn't interested in exploring inside.

Another crazy thing I discovered on our drive south: the dude and I had met once before. I know, insert an Of Course, All Mexicans Are Related joke here. But no, we weren't related. When we were near San Diego, he talked about the time his moms found two illegals hiding in their patio. His family at the time was living right on the edge of the United States, right across from Border Field State Park, a large wetlands area that went right up to the border. Back then it was a popular crossing point because of the scrub that led up to the apartments. D remembered the nightly flyovers by the border patrol in their helicopters with their searchlights cutting through the night and the shadows. So one of these nights, Daniel's mom hears a sound in the patio and walks out to find two men hiding from the border-patrol searchlights. Rather than scream "¡Ilegales!" and slam the door shut, she invited the two inside. One was a younger dude, and his partner was his older brother Diógenes. My tío Diógenes. The younger guy was my pops. He had gone back to bring his brother across. Their plan was to cross over to San Diego and then walk to Irvine over the mountains, avoiding the second border-patrol checkpoint at San Onofre. From there, they would hitchhike to Fowler where we lived.

D's moms heard the story and said, No. No, she repeated. I'll drive you.

And she did. Along with her kids. She told my pops that she wanted to go visit her brothers in Northern California and a side trip to Fowler would be no problem. She just needed a couple of days to plan.

A few days later, my pops and my tío were home with us. I was a kid, so I barely remembered the whole thing other than there was this strange family bringing my dad home.

When D told me the story, I almost turned around to head to Fowler to have him see my family. If it hadn't been for the fact that we were past Oceanside, I would have.

Crazy world.

A few months after Daniel was gone, I ran into la Diabla. I was working at the library that summer, trying to earn some scratch for my move to San Diego for grad school. I was shelving some books when she saw me in the aisle. She came up to me so fast I thought she was going to throw a punch or a kick. I stood back, ready for the onslaught. Instead, she was actually nice to me. Actually treated me like I was human. She wanted to know if I knew anything about D. I had no info, as the bato had not contacted me either.

I hope he finds what he's looking for, she said.

You think he's looking for something? I responded.

Claro. Obviously. She rolled her eyes at me. Finally she said, looking down, Once he realizes what he's got, he's going to be unstoppable.

I just stared at her with the books in my hand. She looked at me, smirked, and gave me a long kiss.

I wasn't expecting that.

She smiled and walked away.

I called out to her, to see if she wanted to go out sometime. She flipped me off.

Cabrona.

La Diabla never could understand why Daniel never tried to make a play for Andrea. But I, in my own fucked up way, understood him completely. There are people like that. They come into your life and before you know it, they've got you. And you can tell yourself that you are in control of your life and your destiny. But when you least expect it, there they are. And when it came to Andrea, he knew that he was not going to have control.

With Betty everything was different. When they were together, he knew that anything was possible. They could either end up naked and sweaty on the floor of the studio or they could be screaming at each other on the street. One time, they hosted this party at a downtown café where they invited local artists and friends and they both traded off as DJs. Shit was bananas. Before the fiesta she cut his hair and did a terrible job at it. He dyed hers and it came out spotty. Another time, for a Halloween party, the two dressed up as Sid and Nancy. Daniel wore leather pants and a T-shirt that said No Future that he changed to No Furniture with a permanent marker. La Diabla bleached her hair and wore a dirty, used wedding dress. They ended up drunk in a booth at Jake's at three in the morning. That was the closest they ever came to being a couple. Another time, they got into a huge agarrón and she ended up insulting him over the air. In the middle of a song she stopped the record and screamed out, This one's for ese hijodeputa Farmer Dan!

But despite all this, when he was with her, he always knew that he had some control. He could leave or he could stay, and there would never be any repercussions. They would always be friends.

With Betty there was no commitment; neither deceived themselves into thinking that they had a future. But with Andrea. Andrea. Daniel knew that he was completely and stupidly stuck. Andrea was danger, peligro, for him. PELIGRO. He knew that he would do anything to always be by her side. And he knew that this would make him suffer. And because of this he decided to leave, to avoid going through that stupid suffering phase.

I know. Fucked up. Completely. Serious pendejismo.

In the end, he suffered. Suffered. Suffered. Suffered. And when he thought he was over it, he suffered some more.

She leaves him her mobile number so he can contact her anywhere in the world. She also gives him a special number for leaving a voice mail. Finally, she writes down her e-mail. Daniel stares at all the numbers and starts to feel dizzy.

The last time he saw la Diabla was in San Diego. He was working for a magazine and he had to interview a local rock singer. The two had spent the morning in Tijuana on a photo shoot and their interview had started while they were sitting in Daniel's car waiting to cross the border. They ended up in a café in Hillcrest where they were talking about lives being marked by border crossing when a familiar voice whispered into his ear, Shall we have a private meeting in the office?

She no longer had the dark punk look. She was wearing a dark-gray suit, and her dark hair was pulled back neatly. It was obvious she was an executive of some sort. They talked a few minutes and then she left him her number to call later. The rocker just stared at them.

Daniel grabbed the napkin where she wrote her number and stuck it in his pocket.

You going to see her, bro? She's fucking hot.

Daniel knew he wasn't going to call. Betty probably knew it too.

Everything changes, he responded to the rocker.

They spend an hour sitting at the bar. Daniel realizes that they barely say anything substantial. Before, Andrea and Daniel could spend hours talking about the music they liked, the movies, the books, whatever. On some afternoons, they would lie on the lawn in front of the administration building and they would talk about their future plans. She imagined herself working in Mexico or some other Latin American country with a group like Greenpeace or an NGO. Daniel couldn't think much beyond the university. He only wanted to live in a city, even though his mom wanted him to move back to his hometown of Orland.

One night as they walked across campus, Andrea took him by the hand. It was a smooth movement, as if her hand were seeking out its natural place. If only things were different, she told him. But she didn't finish. Instead, she began to talk about her astronomy course. She mentioned a class visit to the small observatory on the roof of the science building, a class trip to see the rings of Saturn. She was unimpressed, even a little disappointed, by what she saw. She wanted to see Saturn as shown in the magazines, in bright colors and brilliant beautiful rings.

Saturn isn't like that at all, she said. It's more a dull, caramel color. Space in the movies is much better.

They walked through campus holding hands while she talked. Daniel tried to pay attention, but he was worried that his hand would begin to sweat, that she would let it go, that she would never reach out to touch him again. At some point, Andrea began to talk about their future life together. The two of them doing great work and coming home in the evening. He had no idea what to say.

A week later, he left town after his final radio show.

While she talks about her travels around the world, Daniel wants to ask her if she's happy.

He wants to ask her what she feels when she looks up into the night sky. He wants to know if she feels that space as presented by Spielberg, Lucas, and Kubrick is still more exciting.

He wants to ask if she still likes to dance in her apartment to the music of the Cure.

He wants to ask if she ever missed him.

He wants to ask if she would like to travel with him, to start up again where they had left off.

This time, he thinks, I'll know what to do.

But he doesn't know how to ask.

And she speaks to him of meetings, of international law, of airports.

She looks at her watch and tells him that she has to go.

In that moment, Daniel places his hand on hers. He looks into her eyes. He confesses that he left because he was convinced that he could not add anything to her life. He tells her that he realizes now that it was simply an act of evasion, of running from his emotions, of hiding: he was afraid of commitment. He tells her that he wants to rewind the VCR and go back to spending time with her. Begin again. He wants to invite her to dance.

She looks at her watch and tells him that she has to go.

In that moment, Daniel stares at her. He has no idea how to tell her everything that had crossed his mind. He finds himself like before, without enough words to express everything he wants to say. He can only see himself as a character in a silent movie, trying to talk but with no sound coming out.

She gets up and gives him a long, close hug. She kisses him on the cheek. He can tell that she wants him to say something, anything. He knows that if he asks her to stay, to forget about her flight, to run away with him somewhere else, that she'll accept.

But he doesn't know how to ask.

You know, Andrea says before walking away, the word in Hong Kong for foreigner is *gwui-lo*.

What does that mean?

Ghost, she responds. Then she leans into his ear and whispers, One day I'll tell you the things I've seen.

Lonely Planet

AND THIS IS LIKE a scene out of Cassavetes, out of Jarmusch, out of Rohmer, out of Bujalski. If this were Alphabet City in Manhattan, the Mission in San Francisco, or a random college town like Athens, State College, Ithaca, or Iowa City, this might be the typical hipster story. But since we are watching the rain fall, watching from beneath a fake Mayan arch with the Chiapas selva around us—the hot, humid air mixing with the summer rain dripping down—this is something else. Something.

Mochileros in love.

Mochileros in silence.

Something like that.

And we are standing there, under the buzzing fluorescent light of the hotel portico. Awkward silence pushed between us. In the upstairs lounge of the hotel there are the remnants of a dinner party. The others have left, either crawling back to their rooms or out into the electric Palenque night, looking for their favorite bar in the village. A couple of people, her friends and neighbors, lounge about, talking quietly or staring out the window every time a howler monkey cries into the darkness. The night is heavy, and I am leaving to make my way back to my cheap hostel near the church.

Her hotel is in a designated area of the village where the jungle grows free. The selva here is contained, but a few streets over it is not. And with the effects of the night and the drinks in the lounge, I can feel the selva beyond the village limits wanting to take back the section that is surrounded by buildings and streets. I think of the Mayan ruins on the mountain above us. Of our morning walk with her friends to see the pyramids as the park opened. Of the sun breaking through the clouds as we stood on the Templo de las Inscripciones. Of us, looking out over the selva. Of escaping the heat with a quick dip in the nearby river. Of the hot, sticky, wet heat. Of our descent, tired and exhausted after a day of running around. Of the dinner party that later moved to the lounge. Of sneaky things that can happen in the dark.

Sometimes a lot is said in awkward silences.

We stand close to each other. She tries to tell me not to go, but she is not saying anything. She takes quick glances at me before looking out at the rain.

And there is a great unspoken thing between us.

We are carving big words out of our silence.

Without warning, she punches my arm.

Lying on her bed in Madrid, we used to tell each other stories with the windows open. The sounds from the other apartments: the señora downstairs who sang boleros while making lunch; the couple upstairs who fought every few days, throwing objects, slamming doors, and then the loud, passionate moans that followed as they made up; the guys across the air shaft—two designers for a local magazine—who spent hours playing video games. And beyond the apartment building and its sounds, the traffic that at times seemed to mimic the crashing of waves.

Even then, there were just stories between us: flirting through our anecdotes and pasts. Walking through Malasaña one morning she asked if I would run away with her. I looked at my watch, saying that I would, but I had to be back by three.

Standing in front of the Plaza de los Cubos and considering the long line in front of the Cines Princesa, I suggested we run away to Gijón immediately.

Can't, she responded. I've got a thing with my Cosa at eleven over in Chueca. You can only have me for the next three hours.

I cracked a smile. She looked at me with an arched eyebrow. ¿Y qué? Besides, I think you've also got a thing with your Caos later tonight. In Lavapies, right?

Our partners had no names: they were merely Things, Cosas. Sometimes, most times, they were Caos. And then there were the others that we had flings with, we called them Aves, short for Aventuras. We lived in a story marked by Caos and Aves.

After the movie, we ditched our respective Cosas and wandered around until four in the morning, when I walked her back to her apartment.

Standing in the doorway to her building, she draped her arms around me and looked me straight in the eye. Here it comes, I thought. She leaned forward, then backward, and declared with her eyes narrowed, You really didn't mean that about running away to Gijón. I know your ways, old man.

I had meant it. About running away. But I responded, You're right. I didn't want to run away to Gijón. I meant Lisbon. I hugged her and left.

You're a tease, she sang out after me.

Sorry, I replied. I told the Cosa I'd take her out for breakfast at four thirty.

Madrid doesn't have any all-night diners, Cariño, she reminded me.

Then I guess I'll be making her breakfast in her apartment.

Tease.

This is what we expected from each other. Us: mentirosos, liars, cheaters. What more could there be?

On those visits I never told her that I had flown all night just to feel her by my side.

And at night, back home, separated by a continent and an ocean, wandering around the Mission in San Francisco, I would stop to read the texts that would arrive: her stories of walking around, her funny images of the day that she would see on her strolls around Malasaña, Chueca, Lavapies, La Latina. She wandered the streets and neighborhoods of Madrid with lime-green headphones clamped to her head and a soundtrack that went from ABC to Yello through Blur and Santana. Her online avatar was Maggie from "Mechanics part 2," the pic where she is carrying her tool bag. But to me she looked more like Penny Century crossed with the fierceness of Hopey. Walking together one night to Luke Soy Tu Padre, she bolted after some guy who whistled at her. I continued to the bar and ordered her a beer. When she arrived, she took the glass, smiled, and told me that she had kicked the cabrón near the metro station. I love my new boots, she said.

Often, she would stop and send me a text or, when home, a quick message. So you don't forget me, viejo, she once wrote. Sometimes there would be e-mails from her on her travels as a freelance journalist. From Istanbul she told me about smoking narguila with some Australian mochileros before chiding me for not being there. In Ankara she wrote about a textile collective for *El Comercio.* From Bolivia she sent me a photo. In it she is standing beside a mountain bike and a crazy, winding road cut from the side of a mountain, part of a travel piece about "the most dangerous road in the world" for *La Vanguardia.* From Beirut she told me in one breath about interviewing Lebanese directors and in the other about the nightlife.

How can a Peruana travel so much? I once asked her as we were drinking micheladas at El Alamillo.

Spanish residency, obvio, she responded. What's your excuse, Mr. Chicano?

Made in México, born in the USA, chica.

I would be in the Latin American Club or grabbing a taco at El Farolito and there would be a text from her. She was having breakfast at 7 a.m. after a night out in Madrid, while I would be stepping up to the bar at 10 p.m. in San Francisco. Tell me a story, she would text. Sometimes I would ask whomever I was with to respond. Or, I would lean over and ask some random woman at the bar about the strangest thing she had seen that day. At times I would simply text back: U first.

R asked me 2 marry him!

Is R an Ave or a Cosa?

An Ave! Caos is in Tangiers. Don't u remember anything?

If I asked u 2 marry me, what would u say?

There was no response for an hour. Then:

Going home, had to ditch R in La Latina. Freak. If u did, I would say . . .

And the text ended.

We never admitted anything. Neither wanted to take that first step, hoping secretly that it would be the other to fall, to finally admit what they had been hiding all along. It was a cruel game and we played it well. On a couple of occasions I came close, but caught myself, remembering a story she told me. It was about one of her former professors at the Complutense. She had grown attracted to him over his constant references to music and film and soon they were meeting for café. But her efforts at getting his attention didn't seem to go anywhere; it was just café and nothing more. She took a couple of his classes and still nothing happened. They would flirt back and forth, but he always gave off the impression that it was simply joking. Until he finally cracked one summer week when they both were at El Escorial for separate cursos de verano.

It was great, that Ave, she told me. Until he began to show interest. Real interest. Like he started talking about leaving his wife. Kept talking about us, us together, like a unit. Kept talking about running away with me. And it was no longer a joke. He was serious. Fortunately, I graduated and a job in New York came up. I left. It was always just for fun. But then he wanted a future.

She shuddered, then cracked a smile and looked at me. Don't. Ever. Do. That.

I responded, Hey, don't look at me. I'm just passing through on this lonely planet.

Like those travel guides?

Exactly.

A day later, she sent me a text, inviting me over for dinner at her place:

Just the 2 of us.
                    Still trying to conquer me? I'm not that easy. Try harder.
                    In Barcelona now. Off 2 Mallorca, meeting my Cosa.
Why? Why choose Caos?

We were always so unsure, but at the same time, we weren't. We hid ourselves beneath a facade of stories about our relationships, the flings we'd had, the odd moments we'd witnessed.

———

In the summer of 1988, punk rock broke my heart.

Really?

No. Not really. . . . Well, maybe a little. I think I heard it crack. A bit.

In 1988, I was eight years old.

I was twenty-two.

Old man.

———

I used to be a champion baton twirler. It taught me two things
. . . flexibility.

Yeah?

. . . and concentration.

I watched a lot of TV. Gave me ADD.

———

So we're in this bar in Poble Sec, and we've been drinking red
wine served from these huge barrels. We're having this totally random conversation. . . . I don't know, we're talking about nothing
really. So this woman leans over and whispers in my ear, "Do you
have a girlfriend?" So I lean back and casually glance at her. "I have
a glass of wine . . . and, uh, ten euros." Then I point out a guy at
the bar. "I think he has a girlfriend."

You're so dumb! She was totally into you!

Hey there! I had drinking to do. And you know nothing should
ever come between me and drinking.

Meh. Ok. You got a point there, viejo.

———

In Marrakech I met this Venezolano. A drummer in some anarchist punk band. Long hair. Hot. Love guys with long hair.

Sorry then, guess that's another strike against me. I don't have
long hair.

Oh, well. Grow it out. We'll talk then.

Bueno pues, see you in like . . . never.

Bye.

That was nine months ago. She moved from Spain to Mexico. Cambio de aires, she told me at first. Later she confided that it was because of her Cosa. He told her he loved her. He had started to plan out a future for them. She freaked out and looked for the first job that would get her the fuck out of Spain. Quickly. Palenque came up, documenting the work of a group of archaeologists from the National Institute of Anthropology and History on a project at the ruins. Madrid was a lot of fun but she wanted to check out Chiapas for a while, she told him as she was packing her bags and heading for the airport. He must have realized what she meant, escaping like that. It was the first time he had heard about her trip.

A few months after her arrival, I was on a plane for Mexico. To see her I traveled all night by bus from Mexico City to Villahermosa, before hopping on another bus that would take me to Palenque. I explained to her over the phone that I was working on a project. I could only visit her at most two days. It was all a lie.

Walking down from the ruins she told me about how she left her Cosa. She let him take her to the airport. While waiting for her plane she erased his number from her phone.

That's fucked, I said.

¿Y qué? Like you would not have done the same thing.

She had me there. I remembered how I broke up with my Cosa: sent an e-mail and set any replies from her to go directly to my junk mail. I also changed her ring tone on my phone to one of a loud alarm. Danger, danger, Will Robinson, I would think whenever she called, and I would never answer.

She knew I had no response and began to laugh. Soon I did too. We laughed our way down the mountain.

And I look at her, in the buzzing light of the hotel portico while we wait for the rain to stop. Two cheaters standing in the rain afraid to confess. I put my arm around her and she rests her head on my shoulder. It feels so natural. I rest my chin on her hair. I want to tell her that I want to stay. Or maybe I want us to be like this. I want to tell her to run away with me. To wherever, anywhere. But that other part of me, the part that always stops me, tells me that she is a bad bet. She's told me her stories. I know her past. I know her. Living completely in the present, she can't conceive the future as anything more than a straightjacket on her desires. She wants to be able to go in so many directions at once. And I know this because I am the same way. I have always bombed in relationships because of my failure to commit. And this failure reveals itself over and over again in every affair I end over e-mail or distance, burying me deeper in my own personal history of ruin.

And there we are, standing in the portico under the steady rain: two people afraid of being close for too long; two people unsure of where to go. Carving out a story together in gaps and pauses. Speaking without saying anything.

And I watch the falling rain, the few people walking home after a night out, the amber lights of Palenque. I'm worn down. Always so unsure. On nights like this we realize we are both only playing a part in a movie that seems to have no direction: something like Cassavetes, something like Jarmusch, something like Rohmer, something like Bujalski.

And later, back in San Francisco, I wake up sweating in bed, convinced that I am going to die alone in my apartment, that no one will come and my body will lay there rotting for months. In the dark, I think of her. I imagine that she is off adventuring deeper into the selva, wandering up to San Cristobal de las Casas, drifting among the Maya. And I realize that I miss her. And I wish I had not left the way that I had: that I had not basically told her good-bye in a long message a few days after my return. Her reply hadn't seemed to acknowledge what I had sent, aside from a couple of random sentences. The first was between stories about meeting with some anthropologists. I don't know what I've done to deserve you, she wrote. And later, after a brief story about a day trip to Agua Azul, she ended her message: I never had a chance to explain exactly what I felt.

Carmen Whose Last Name
I Don't Remember

CARMEN WHOSE LAST NAME I don't remember lives in a house far from here. I sit on the beach listening to the waves and to the cars cruising along the boardwalk. She walks by me, oblivious to the long stares of the young batos as she passes aimlessly near the crashing waves in her skirt, white top, and sun hat. I watch her walk: past a young girl digging a wall in the sand with a shovel; past a man holding a baby who wants to leap from his arms into the water; past a dark-haired woman posing for a photograph with the crashing waves as a backdrop; past me burying my feet into the sand.

Carmen? I ask. And the waves answer, No. And the cars cruising the boardwalk answer, No. And the young batos on the beach answer, No. And the girl digging a wall in the sand answers, No. And the man holding the baby answers, No. And the dark-haired woman posing for the photograph answers, No. And my feet dig a deeper hole into the sand.

No.

Carmen whose last name I don't remember has green eyes that look at me from across a room. Full red lips that whisper my name in the silence of the hotel room near the zócalo. The room, like the many others we passed through, had nothing on the walls. Shoulder-length, wavy brown hair that is often tied back in a tight bun. Pale, translucent skin that she consciously shades from the sun as we sit under an umbrella on the rooftop restaurant of the Hotel Majestic.

What more can I tell you about Carmen? At first I thought that homegirl was a fresa, one of those niñas bien from Lomas or Tecamachalco whose life was lived behind thick walls, with large garden parties frequented by the Mexico City elite and shopping trips to expensive malls in Dallas or Houston and very little contact with anyone outside of her social class: contact with people like me, for example.

I arrived in Mexico City at the end of spring, having enrolled in a summer program at the Universidad Iberoamericana, a private university on the edge of the city. After my first year of grad school in Santa Barbara, my primary desire was to get the fuck out of California for a time, and I found a program that sounded promising. I considered going back to Oaxaca, where I had lived for a few years, but I decided I wanted to check out Mexico City for a while.

When I first set foot on campus, I was convinced I had made the wrong choice. The Benzes and the BMWs in the student parking lot were a clue to the social class that I was entering. As I walked across campus in search of the international students office, I noticed a group rating people with numbered signs. Heading up the stairs to the office, I passed a dude wearing a T-shirt that declared: It's not who you are, it's what you wear. At the top, I looked at my scuffed jeans and sneakers, and old, faded shirt. I stopped at the landing and looked out over the central patio and watched the students in their clean, fashionable clothes. They reminded me of the idiots Lalo used to talk about at Dartmouth.

It was going to be a rough summer.

It was in one of my literature classes that I met Julián and Marcos. Julián was the son of a senator, and Marcos's father was the governor of a northern Mexican state. It was at one of our work meetings that Marcos invited us to the opening of a new video bar in Polanco. At first I declined; I hated that scene. But I finally decided to go because I needed to meet people. There was a thick crowd around the bar when we arrived, but one of the doormen saw Marcos and quickly ushered us inside. The crowd parted, and the black velvet rope was opened. Inside, we made the rounds. They were both greeting friends. I followed, not knowing anybody and feeling like I'd been teleported to the wrong planet. At a table in the corner, where only the center of the table was illuminated, Marcos stopped to introduce everyone.

Carmen, his voice said, as a hand reached out to mine through the darkness.

In a hotel room with a blue ceiling, I heard the shower turning off. I lay on the bed with the rumpled blue sheets and the squeaking springs, staring up at the ceiling, a thin path of light piercing through the curtains. Carmen, wrapped in a faded white towel that, like the sheets, spoke of dubious pasts and repeated washings, came out of the bathroom and jumped onto the bed next to me. Carmen, you smell of cheap soap here on the nape of your neck, here where your hair meets your skin; here on your shoulder blade; here on the small of your back.

You're bad, she said. Stop it. She rolled over and fixed me with that gaze that always caused me to stop and catch my breath.

At a party two weeks later we ran into each other. Carmen wore long fake eyelashes and a painted mole by her left eye. I'm feeling Fellini-esque tonight, she whispered in my ear, grazing my neck with her red lips as she passed by me in the hall on her way to join a group of friends. I headed into another room. There was a large map of the city on the wall. I could feel Carmen's eyes on my back. Before turning, I traced the streets, hotels, cafés, and bookstores that made up our city, the city that we made for ourselves in our wanderings around. Here, in a too-loud video bar on Masarik, we first met. Here, on the corner of the university, we saw each other for the first time after the video bar. Here, at the rooftop restaurant of the Hotel Majestic, overlooking the central plaza, we watched a political demonstration. Here, in a used bookstore on Donceles, we ran into each other on a summer Saturday as we both reached for the same book. Here, in a cheap hotel near there, we escaped our first summer downpour, the first in a series of cheap hotels and summer afternoons, some rainy, some not.

On the red-eye I think about this and I think about that and I think, What if I hadn't left? My thoughts and memories float out over the midnight clouds.

I remembered the flight from the first time I went to the city. I thought of the jet that had fallen from the sky a year earlier. Back then my greatest fear was to be in an airline accident. I sat nervously in the seat, waiting for the takeoff. As we flew through the clouds, I felt the plane groan, followed by a loud clap as the jet began to shake. I grabbed the armrests harder as a hole opened by my side, and then I was sucked out into the sky. I plummeted through those clouds, intact and alert, while pieces of jet fell around me. My eyes were opened wide as I rushed headfirst toward that city of streets and buildings and ruins and people.

I was asleep before the plane left the runway. When I awoke, we were landing in Mexico City.

The decision to leave California had been quick: a few months earlier I suddenly announced that I wanted to go to Mexico City. My family in Orland thought I was fucking nuts. Especially my tío Chavo. He couldn't stand the arrogance of the people from the capital; the Chilangos felt that everything outside of Mexico City was a provincial backwater. To my relatives, the capital was a monstrous city, overpopulated, contaminated, and the center of all that was wrong in the country. Silvia was convinced that I was leaving because our brief relationship had exploded. Lucía, my side girl, was convinced I was leaving because she had found out about Silvia. Santa Barbara was too small for those kinds of shenanigans. I could never figure out how my tocayo Daniel was able to pull that shit off. A few of the familias in Orland were certain that I was leaving because the town was cursed following my primo Todd's death. A number of high school students were killed in stupid accidents, and people began to look for reasons. Some of my Chicano friends thought I was going to deepen my relationship to the raza.

Lalo, Todd's brother, was the only one who recognized my need for distance. I didn't go to Mexico to hide from the two exes who found out about each other, or to escape our hometown's superstitions. Nor did I go seeking my roots. I simply woke up one morning with the thought: I should go to Mexico City.

I never expected to meet Carmen.

Carmen whose last name I don't remember smiles from a photograph. She sits in an outdoor café, a glass of wine in her hand. Her hair is tied back with a green ribbon. She wears a black linen shirt. I replace the photo inside the book where I've been carrying it and look out the window of the plane and imagine the countryside passing below.

Carmen?

And a woman in a black dress and mirrored sunglasses reflecting the eyes of someone who's just traveled all night by plane responds, No.

When I arrived in Mexico City that time, I walked out of the airport terminal carrying an old battered backpack with some books, my journal, and a beat-up camera I had bought for cheap. A tattered black shoulder bag carried my clothes, and in my wallet was all the money that I had in the world. Still half-asleep, I stood on the sidewalk and watched the sun rising over the city. My senses were assaulted: my nose assailed by diesel fumes from the trucks and the buses; my ears bombarded with music playing from the open windows of the traffic-filled streets; my mouth filled with the metallic taste of taxis weaving through the traffic as they pushed their way past walls of billboards. The sky was gray and hazy and I was tired from an all-night flight and I really had no idea where I was going to stay as people ran all around me, everyone burdened with their suitcases.

And I leaned against the wall and tried to figure out where to go. After a few minutes, I pulled my shit together and took a taxi, asking to be dropped off in the city center. On the way, the driver and I struck up a conversation and he suggested a hotel. In the centro, cheap, he told me. I stayed there a few weeks while I looked for a place to live.

Stepping out of the terminal, I see the cars lined up; I see the taxis weaving through the traffic; I see the people rushing past; I see the gray, hazy day; I see four pigeons; I don't see Carmen.

A taxi takes me to the same hotel where I first arrived years earlier.

Was it the most idiotic thing in the world to return to Mexico City after fifteen years to find someone whose last name I don't remember? Yes. Stupid. Idiotic. Dumb.

But here I am.

Let's see, this line here on your palm states that you will never leave Mexico City.

This one?

Yes, that crooked one.

I don't tell her that in my pocket I have the confirmation number for my departure flight.

The city offered me anonymity. In the evenings I would sit at the dining table, the window open so that I could hear the street sounds. My favorite activity, though, was to walk. Back then it was safe to walk at night. The city offered me endless possibilities for walking; I could easily lose myself in those strolls.

Don't get me wrong. I had been back to the city. The first time was three years after leaving, back when I became serious about grad school. I had some work to do at the campus of UNAM and in that week I spent in the library I never once thought of her. A couple of years after that, I was back, this time with Magda. We were only here for a few days, though; our plans were to go to Oaxaca for two weeks. We rented an apartment and spent the nights walking around the plaza. Things were good then. Lots of sex. We were sticky with it. But as she would say, that was then.

So, one afternoon I'm down on the beach, trying to avoid going home. Magda had left. For good this time. She always said that. This time I think she meant it. And though I had done all I could to get her to stay—the begging, the crawling, the apologizing for all past, present, and future transgressions, the promises to be better—she still packed her bags and walked out. She did this the morning after we had a truly spectacular day together: we walked on the beach in the morning, I made a lunch that was so good even I was surprised, we walked hand-in-hand around downtown. Looking at our reflections in the window of a bookstore I said, Damn, we look good together. And we did. She agreed. The night ended with wine at this fancy bar that always made me feel nervous and out of place among the designer-label crowd.

Magda, though, she loved that shit.

The next morning, she was gone. Before walking out the door she told me that was how she wanted to remember us: looking good together.

Lying on the beach, I heard someone yell out, Carmen! Then I thought, Why not? Why not take a trip to Mexico City?

The rain caught us by surprise. We had just left the café at the Templo Mayor and were looking at the ruins of the Aztec main temple on Donceles when the skies darkened. She offered me a ride home and we began to walk briskly toward her car. In front of a cheap hotel, she stopped. Why don't we wait in here? she asked, a crooked smile on her face. As we walked up to our room, I wanted to tell her that I had stayed in this same hotel when I arrived in the city.

Carmen?

And a woman in front of the old hotel off Donceles where we first spent a summer downpour responds, No.

The hotel has changed little since that rainy Saturday. The entry is still dark and a bored younger woman has replaced the bored young woman who took our money at the reception desk. The room still smells of disinfectant. The only change is that now the bare room is decorated with a painting, to make it inviting, I guess. I take it down, then step out into the day.

The taxi passes the Monument to the Revolution and I see the taquería where Carmen and I once ran into each other. It was crowded and I had been waiting some time for service when I felt her breath on my neck. She kissed my neck and asked if I'd ordered her a soda. What flavor? Red, she stated to me, Red, she said to the waiter who nodded his head. Red.

Another summer afternoon, and we were in the centro without our umbrellas. We stood on the corner under the canopy of a book-store hoping to catch a taxi before the rain came down harder. It was a Sunday and no taxis came. There's a hotel nearby, I offered. She looked at me and smiled before taking my arm.

You planned this. Only now it's your turn to pay, she declared.

Ours was a story of chance meetings. I'd be stepping out of the post office near Bellas Artes and there she would be, in her car, waiting for the light. I'd be walking out of the main library at the university and she would be coming in. I'd be eating at the lunch bar in La Blanca and turn to find her next to me in conversation with someone else.

I'd be in Gandhi bookstore, checking out the menu in the café, and then there'd she'd be, sitting at my table, pulling off her black beret, taking off her leather shoulder bag, unbuttoning her dark green coat, and smiling at me. Carmen at Bellas Artes studying the colors in the mural by Camarena, following the lines, attempting to penetrate the translucent layers of color, and then me sneaking up behind her. Carmen and I running into each other by the flower clock in the sunken park.

Amazing how in a city of this size we keep bumping into each other. You must be following me, I said to her. No, it's fate, was her sarcastic reply as her car glided through traffic on Universidad, heading toward Coyoacán.

In an outdoor café, I sit with a book and watch the people walk by, enjoying a Sunday in the plaza of Coyoacán.

Carmen? I ask

And a woman selling handmade jewelry looks up.

Carmen?

Who?

She is a woman whose last name I don't remember. She is a woman who loves art. She is a woman who loved this city. She is a woman who I never really thought of while I lived here. She is a woman who has always been on my mind since I left, even though I forgot her last name, even though I lost her address years ago, even though I left without saying good-bye.

Carmen?

No. But I see instead the vendors selling their wares; the people enjoying a Sunday in Coyoacán; the cars passing by; the church; the sky. And she views me with eyes hidden behind sunglasses and beads in her hair, with a peace symbol hanging from one ear while the Aztec Sun Stone hangs from the other.

My decision to leave was as abrupt as my decision to come to the city. The night before, Carmen and I had dinner at a taquería on Insurgentes. I didn't tell her I was leaving.

Carmen?

A woman responded.

A woman who I once knew: it was Malena.

Carmen?

No. I haven't seen her in years, though she still might be here. You know how big this city is. The last time I saw her was at the Casa de los Azulejos. In her hands she had her shoulder bag. She was just leaving Sanborn's with a friend. She saw me, said hi, asked how I was, and then said good-bye. They had someone waiting. I watched them walk out the door, turn in the direction of the zócalo, and disappear into the afternoon crowds.

I stand in the entryway of the Sanborn's on Madero looking toward the zócalo on a day like the one years ago, the day that saw Carmen leave Sanborn's and pass the children selling gum, the woman on the corner with her child in her rebozo, the guard with his machine gun at the jewelry store.

I head toward the central plaza, past the people who saw her that day.

Malena, who was stopping into Sanborn's, saw her.

A businessman who lived in a penthouse in Polanco saw her.

A woman who washed clothes in Colonia Guerrero saw her.

The newspaper vendor on the corner of Madero and 5 de Mayo saw her.

I didn't see her then.

Fifteen Volkswagen taxis by the zócalo. I count the green bochos as I count the seconds running off of my time left here, as I count the number of stories in this city, stories of which mine is a part: stories sinking into the mud below, blending into the layers of silt, shifting into the rock, mixing with the artifacts of lost cultures. And I think about the woman who I spent four months with: three months, three weeks, and six days, to be exact, though I don't know how I came to that number, how I counted. I walk to the map of what the Aztec capital looked like when the Spaniards arrived. I study the bridges linking the floating city to the mainland. I try to imagine what part of that city I am standing on now.

Here, on this corner of the Main Temple, Carmen kissed my forehead as we waited in line to get into the museum.

Carmen?

No one answers.

I walk the streets of the colonial downtown, tracing out prior steps on the markings of millions of other footsteps.

Here is where Carmen and I once glanced into the window of a shoe store. I had commented that one of the things that surprised me about this part of the city was the absence of grocery stores. There were so many shoe stores. I wondered what the people survived on. Shoes of course, Carmen responded. Watch the register; if you stare long enough you will see that when the woman working at the register thinks she's not being watched, she'll slide a shoestring into her mouth. She feels lucky on those days when she can stuff a whole leather shoe into her cheeks. I marveled at her absurdity, but we looked nonetheless. The woman at the register caught us staring. We walked away laughing. There is where Carmen and I once waited for a taxi when she was left without a car. On that corner, I bought the Saturday edition of *Unomásuno*. In that bookstore, I found a copy of Guillermo Samperio's *Gente de la ciudad*.

As the rain began to fall we stepped into the Café de Tacuba. This is my favorite place to have morning coffee, she told me. Carmen smiled as the waitress poured steaming milk into a glass. She then took the decanter of black liquid from the table and poured a few drops into the milk. We ordered some pan dulce to go with our coffee. While she read the paper, I looked over the calendar of activities in the cultural supplement, though my Saturdays rarely varied. We would walk back to the lot where her car was parked or, if she had come without it, to the street to grab a taxi. She would then get in her car or taxi and head off. I would walk to the metro station and head for the Chopo. Then, as I'd be leaving the weekly musical swap meet, I'd find her sitting on the hood of her car, talking to some musicians.

Carmen looking through a telescope on the observation deck of the Latin American tower. Tell me what you see, I said. I see a man in a red shirt eating a taco and a woman in a blue dress drinking a red drink and they don't know each other. I see a young boy selling gum on the street. I see a tired woman in a blue rebozo resting her head in her hands on the steps at the Palace of Fine Arts. I see a man and a woman sharing a mango and making plans in the Alameda park. I see a young man writing in a green notebook. I see a woman in a black skirt and white top with short hair walking past a group of workmen who try to grab her attention, but she keeps walking forward. I see a man who spits flames out of his mouth, a woman who sells candy, a child who cleans windshields; I see a city that goes on forever.

She slowly ate her churro; we were in El Moro having a late-night snack of churros and hot chocolate. She ran a hand through her hair as she told me about how when she was young her parents used to come here in the mornings. My father would read *Excélsior*, my mother would fuss over me, telling me to be careful and not to spill any chocolate on my dress. But now, she looked down at her chocolate, they never come downtown. Their city is over there; over here is too old.

Carmen whose last name I don't remember was discussing a play with a journalist over café con leche and banderillas at the Café Habana. This city is much more than an apocalyptic night-mare, much more than smog and corruption, she declared, whip-ping her cigarette in the air. The city, here, is still very much alive. I watched the people who walked past, the yellow Volkswagen taxis on their way to Reforma, the smell of roasting coffee in the air. It was late in the morning, hazy light filtered in through the large windows, and I watched Carmen criticizing the vision of the city that the play presented. She didn't care that the writer was sitting at a table near ours. I walk past the Habana, looking in briefly to see if Carmen and I are sitting at the table in the corner, laughing over some old joke. Instead, there is a group of journalists sitting at the table. I make my way to Reforma, crossing Morelos past a large number of green Volkswagen taxis.

Carmen, this city is a circus. Yes, but what a great one.

We never made plans to meet, but sometimes the coincidence was too much. I'd be stepping out of my apartment building in the evening and there she'd be, slipping out of the darkness with her hair pulled back, her pale luminous skin, and her red lips. The first few times the effect of her materializing before me was unnerving.

We would walk to her car and I would say, Where do you want to go? Surprise me, she'd reply, turning on the car, though I knew that she had already made up her mind. I was always the one who'd be surprised as Carmen led me through the different paths that make up this city. Maybe we'd go to LUCC or to Rockotitlán to see the latest rock bands. Maybe we'd go to the Bar León to listen to salsa, or go dancing at the Salón California.

We'd always end in a cheap hotel somewhere in the city center.

We each had our own homes. Mine was an apartment near the British Embassy; it was on the fifth floor of a six-story building. My bedroom window looked out over a large circle that is listed on the city maps as Plaza Necaxa. In reality, it was a large paved space with no markings, where two streets intersected. One night, Julián, Marcos, and I made paper airplanes and tried to throw them across the circle. The next morning, I walked out to find them in the trees.

From across the street, I look up at the window that was once mine. The doorman's wife steps out of the building, I find it hard to believe she still lives there. I watch her as she crosses Plaza Necaxa in the direction of the grocery store a few blocks down. In the window that used to be mine I see someone looking out over the plaza. I turn and head in the direction of Reforma.

Where were you when the earthquake hit?

Home in bed. Later, I was working in one of the shelters. It was terrible.

She tells me how during an earthquake in the 1950s the Angel fell from her column. It was a Friday evening and we were sitting on a stone bench on Reforma facing the traffic circle of the Angel of Independence. There is a stairway that runs up through the column to the feet of the Angel. It has been closed for years. In the fifties the views from there must have been incredible, Carmen said. On the corner we watched a family performing for change at the traffic light. At the red light, the father stepped out into the intersection, drank from a bottle of clear liquid, held up a torch, and spit flames into the night. His young children walked among the cars collecting money. Their mother sat on the island between the lanes selling paper flowers. We got up from the bench and continued to walk down Reforma in the direction of Chapultepec. When we passed the family, we left them all the change we were carrying.

Carmen whose last name I don't remember lives in a large house on the edge of the city, in Las Lomas. Her father was a businessman always away, her mother a socialite who was often mentioned in the society pages. I was at her house twice. I was standing outside of the university waiting for the bus when she pulled up in her car. Her hair was pulled back in a bun, her bright-red lips floated on the surface of her pale skin. She offered me a ride home. But first I have to stop by my house, she said. It took me a moment to remember her as the woman I had met a few nights earlier. At her house, I waited in the living room while she dropped off her books and made a phone call. Then she drove me home before heading out into the Friday evening to meet some friends at a bar near the zócalo. Do you want to come? Sorry, I can't. Kiss on the cheek. Thanks for the ride. No problem, I'll see you around. I stood outside my building and watched her drive away.

At a party at her house I stood out on the balcony overlooking the pool. I could hear her father in his office telling a group of people how privatizing the national industries would bring about a new age of prosperity for the country. Carmen, who had been mingling among the guests with her mother, joined me with a rum and coke in her hand. She rolled her eyes when she heard what her father was saying. A photographer who I'd had a conversation with a few weeks earlier at the Habana came up to take a photo of us for the newspaper. We left soon after and headed for a bar in the Colonia Roma. Later we were in another cheap hotel near the Monument to the Revolution, groping around in the dark.

We were sitting in a taquería when she stated, You know, if you were to leave I wouldn't be sad.

Really?

Because I know that you'll be back. Maybe it would be a long time, maybe a few weeks.

Maybe never.

No, you'll come back.

Carmen, I have a flight that leaves in the morning, I didn't tell her. She stared out the window at the passing cars.

Carmen whose last name I don't remember and I in our four months together made the rounds of the cheap hotels in the city. In the bare rooms, we escaped the summer rains by spending those afternoons or nights in beds that were always the same: old, hard, and of dubious pasts. At times, she would sleep and I would lie under the covers and listen to the rain, that constant rain coming down upon the city outside the hotel window, that rain that comes down upon me now as I walk through the Alameda park.

Carmen? I ask.

And a young girl walking past with her parents answers, No.

Carmen?

I ask: a woman working in a record store; a watchman at Bellas Artes; a traffic cop on Eje Central; a woman posing for a photograph on the observation deck at the Latin American Tower with the Alameda park as a backdrop.

No.

I ask: a tired woman with two children on the metro; a man reading a newspaper; a policewoman at the Tlatelolco plaza watching a child walk with her parents; a woman working the ticket booth at Metro La Villa.

No.

I ask: a penitent man on his knees at the basilica; a young girl eating a strawberry popsicle near the doors to the small church on the hill of Tepeyac; the Virgen of Guadalupe.

No.

To be with her was to be in a chaos of colors, of sounds, of images. Carmen whispering into my ear about the rudeness of the kissing couple on the bench at the gardens of the Basilica of Guadalupe. Carmen biting on my ear when I laughed at another of her whispered suggestions as we stepped off the grounds. Carmen putting on her red lipstick before getting out of the car. Carmen kissing my forehead in the morning to wake me up.

Driving around the city, Marcos and I stop at a bank machine near her home. While we're waiting in the car, Carmen passes by. I know she sees me, but she doesn't acknowledge my presence. Later that night we run into each other in La Guadalupana bar. She makes no mention of my being in her neighborhood. As we step out into the darkness of Coyoacán, she whispers, Never come looking for me. I'll always find you.

In a crowded bar I saw her in the corner with some friends who are chatting about who was going out with whom. She sat in the booth quietly, twisting the ring with the emerald stone on her finger. As I walked by, she grabbed my arm. Let's dance, she said. After dancing, I asked if she wanted to go back to her friends.

No, you see, my friends are boring me to tears, tearing me to shreds, shredding me to pieces, piecing me to bits, and biting me in places I don't want to be bit. You know what I mean? I tried to unravel it as she aimed reflected light from her emerald ring onto my face. Let's leave, besides I don't know those people, friends of my sister's, you know, doing the family thing, she said in one sentence. Where to? I asked. Surprise me, she replied. Just let me pay this time, she told me as we left the bar.

In the darkened hotel room, my ringing phone awakens me from a dream. I pick up the receiver hearing the falling rain outside and ask, half-asleep, Carmen? There is a silence of static on the line as I wait for a reply from Carmen whose last name I don't remember.

Manhattan Transfer

SOMETIMES MOVIES COME TO you at just the right moment. Like books. Like certain songs. A few months ago, in an English-language bookshop in Istanbul—the one on Divan Yolu Caddesi near the Sultanahmet tram stop whose name escapes me—Onur grabbed my arm in surprise. You've never seen *Manhattan*? Kamil and he had been talking about the film while I flipped through books. When I mentioned that I hadn't seen it, both of them looked surprised. On a previous trip we caught a couple of Woody Allen films—*Annie Hall, Sleeper, Deconstructing Harry, Match Point*—but we missed the showing of *Manhattan*.

Lalo, *canim*. You must see it, Kamil insisted.

The film came in the familiar red envelope a few days ago. As I was busy finishing a couple of projects for my cultural geography courses, I was unable to see it until tonight.

It made me remember Amanda.

She was young, eighteen, when we first met. I was teaching then at San Francisco State. Thirty-six years old and recently divorced.

The job offer came at an opportune moment: I was in need of distance from New York City where my wife and I had met, got married, and lived. Over on Amsterdam, near the Cathedral of St. John the Divine. She was a young lawyer moving up and I was lecturing at Columbia in geography. We loved walking around Manhattan, especially in the early evening. We would often go to the movies and afterward stop into whatever diner or café we came across to talk. Woody Allen was one of our favorite directors. Though we were both from migrant working families in California, his stories of the privileged classes in Manhattan always struck us as exotic and somehow alien; they were dispatches from a world to which we had little access. The New York City that we inhabited was nothing like his.

After the divorce—we shared certain things in common, certain movies, certain books, certain songs, but the bedrock things, those necessary things, we didn't—I stopped watching his films. Maybe because I realized that as she rose up in the ranks at her job our lives were beginning to approximate his stories. We were living in *Crimes and Misdemeanors, Husbands and Wives,* or *Manhattan Murder Mystery*: cruel films with relationships in crisis that mirrored our own. A few months after the divorce I began to watch *Husbands and Wives* but stopped a third of the way into it because I started crying. When she was upset she used to complain that I didn't know how to cry, that I had no emotions, that I lacked empathy. I sat there on my beat-up sofa with the TV off while large tears rolled down my face. I looked out the window of my rented studio in Brooklyn and stared into the empty yard below. There was a light on in the apartment across the way, but I didn't see anyone. I knew then that it was time to leave New York.

One of the reasons I never watched *Manhattan* was because I was sure it would bring back memories of her. Instead, I thought of

Amanda, whom I met in San Francisco. We met at Muddy Waters when I was sitting alone reading a book, and she came by and asked if I wouldn't mind sharing the table. We started talking when I noticed she was carrying a book by a friend of mine. She had brownish-blonde hair, her favorite band was Tender Trap, and she was studying art history. The incredible awkward Amanda, tall, long-necked, and skinny. She was prone to tripping into things. More than once I caught her just as she was about to take a spill, and it is pretty common knowledge that I am a man of little grace. When I walk, I appear to fight the air. And though Amanda put on a good show of fluidity in movement, there would be moments when a slight wind, a bump in the sidewalk, a sign that would catch her eye, would be enough to bring crashing down the facade of being cool and in control

I found all of this charming about her. I called her la awkwardorable Amanda.

She loved me since the day she met me. Or so she claimed that first night we got together, nearly two years after we met, when she was twenty and I was staring at thirty-eight with a look of bewilderment because it seemed so close to forty. Before that, we maintained a lengthy correspondence through e-mail and text message. At the beginning of my second year at SF State, I was given a fellowship by the Council of American Overseas Research Centers to do some work in Istanbul. In the months leading up to my move, Amanda often stopped by my office to talk. For the summer she went home to Atwater, a small, central valley farming community near Merced and Fresno. She would send me lengthy daily e-mails, talking about her life and the things she would see as she walked around the small town. Sometimes she would send me text messages.

In Istanbul, I looked forward to her messages. Given the ten-hour time difference, I would often get messages from her in the morning as I was getting ready to work at the research center and she was about to go out for the night. She loved to make lists and ask hypothetical questions. The texts would often ask me to describe my morning in five adjectives, or to choose a superpower that didn't involve flight. In another, she told me she was thinking of running off with a trucker so she could see the country from the cab of a long-haul trailer. She once sent me a list of foods and asked me to tell her whether I liked them or not. Another time, she described a conversation she overheard while standing in line for a movie at the Red Vic. Other messages would talk about her favorite bands—she was partial to K Records—Tiger Trap ("Puzzle Pieces" was one of her favorite songs), Beat Happening, Mecca Normal, Kimya Dawson, Heavenly, the Softies. From the Bay Area, she loved the Thinking Fellers Union Local 282.

Her messages describing the places where she would hang out, the music she was listening to, the bands she was seeing, the books she was reading, made me feel that I was still a part of that city though I was living in a tiny apartment over on the Asian shore of Istanbul. When I walked out of my building, I wasn't in the Mission District of San Francisco, I was in Kadıköy, and instead of Spanish I was hearing Turkish.

And through it all, it never occurred to me that her messages could have a deeper meaning. It wasn't until that night, three months after my return, when we drove from San Francisco to Stanford because it suddenly occurred to us that we wanted to see the Gates of Hell at the Rodin sculpture garden. We drove through a thunderstorm without thinking that maybe walking around the Stanford campus at night in the rain would be a bad idea. Amanda had never seen the sculpture, and I had seen the one at the Rodin Museum in Paris. By the time we got to campus, the rain had stopped. After seeing the Gates of Hell we went to visit the Burghers of Calais. We walked around them before standing in the middle of the circle that they formed. She hugged me and we kissed.

We're so cheesy, she said, before kissing me again.

Later that night, after a one-in-the-morning taco run in the Mission district, we walked hand in hand down Mission Street toward 16th. From that night on, we were often together. Walking around the Haight. Lounging on the lawn in Golden Gate Park. Walking around the Palace of the Legion of Honor in the fog. Stumbling around the ruins of the Sutro Baths. Exhibits at the Museum of Modern Art, the Mexican Museum, the Galería de la Raza. Shows at the Fillmore, the Warfield, Bimbo's. Pizza in North Beach. Tacos in the Mission. Coffee in the Richmond.

It was all so comfortable.

But she was so young and I felt that she had a lot of things—experiences, travel, people to meet—that she needed to do before falling into any kind of serious relationship. I tried to remain unattached, to remind her that this was only a temporary fling. And she would remind me of the things we held in common, not just the simple things but the serious, core things.

Eight months after our fling had begun, I pushed her away. To heal my wounded heart, I took a visiting position for a year in Mexico City. A month into living there she sent me an e-mail with a song attached, Stars's "Reunion." The subject was "I want to show how you were right for me." There was no other message. I never responded.

I thought I had pushed her away because she really needed to move on to other more exciting things, to live other experiences, to be with someone closer to her age. In reality I did it because I was afraid that she would realize precisely that. She would leave me first. And I wasn't ready for that. I wasn't ready to be left again.

A year later, when I next saw her, she was in a relationship. We met for coffee in the Sunset and she told me about her boyfriend. They were serious, she claimed repeatedly. Serious. All the while, she looked at me accusingly, wondering how I could have let her go. And though we didn't say it, the feelings remained between us. I knew that if I were to make a play for her again, she would leave her boyfriend without a thought. But I didn't say anything.

A few days later, she sent me a text message saying that she couldn't see me anymore. She still carried a lot of feelings for me, but she was determined to make her relationship work. I wished her well.

We continued to send messages, but they soon grew further and further apart. In the beginning, I would send her a text and would often get a rapid response. In the end, more often than not, I got nothing. Until finally she stopped responding altogether.

Lying on my red couch, watching *Manhattan* in the small Iowan town where I now lived, I didn't think of my ex-wife and the city that we lived in, but rather of Amanda, the wacky young woman who was a part of my life and a part of that city by the Pacific. Watching the towers of Manhattan in stunning black and white, I remembered the bright lights of Market Street on a January night, steam rising from the vents under the street, the crowds out shopping, and Amanda and me sitting on a bench watching it all. Had I seen *Manhattan* before, I might've lifted a line of dialogue and told her—like Woody Allen does to Mariel Hemingway in the back of a carriage going through Central Park—"You know what you are? You're God's answer to Job, y'know? You would have ended all argument between them. I mean, He would have pointed to you and said, y'know, 'I do a lot of terrible things, but I can still make one of these.' You know? And then Job would have said, 'Eh. Yeah, well, you win.'"

Despedidas

CLARA. THIS IS HOW I remember her. She was taller than me. She had long, curly, blonde hair, white skin, and big blue eyes, and she wore a short, blue dress. Her legs were skinny and on her doll feet she wore white socks and tennis shoes.

Clara. She arrived one August day on my sister Diana's fifth birthday and Mamá proudly shouted, ¡Hija! A new friend for you! Diana and I both ran to the front door and there she was, Clara, smiling next to a large gift box.

Clara. I hadn't thought about her since the last time I spoke with Diana. This was a couple of months ago, right after I got back from Turkey.

Clara. For years I had nightmares of that blonde giant who chased us around the house. She had an awkward gait and her arms were often outstretched: her walk reminded me of either Frankenstein's monster or a robot. Clara's arms wanted to hug us but we weren't having any of that shit and we would start to run whenever she appeared.

Our parents would crack up when they saw how we reacted around Clara. ¡Aquí viene! I would shout. Here she comes! Diana would scream. ¡La monstrua! And then we would run. Two little brown Mexican kids in fear of the tall white girl. El jefe would put his cerveza down and nearly fall on the floor from laughing. La jefa would double over and wipe tears from her eyes as she watched us.

Mamá, la jefa, loved her. Loved loved loved her. She would brush Clara's golden locks. She would make her dresses, and she would give her all the love that el jefe could not provide to la jefa because he worked too long at the dairy. That and the fact that he often made a long, long stop at the cantina on his way home.

Clara's presence in the house seemed to be good for Mamá. El jefe had crossed the border for work a few months after I was born in a hospital on the California side of the line. He often did the twelve-hour drive from Northern California to Baja California to see us. After one trip where the Mustang broke down near Fresno and he almost missed work, we joined el jefe for good in El Norte. Diana was born a few months later. And though they were originally illegal and it was the late '60s when life for Mexicanos was pretty fucked, they got lucky. Orland, the town where they landed in Northern California, had a large Mexicano community. There was a lot of work on the farms, in the peach and orange groves, in the olive orchards, and in the dairies. They both labored in the orchards until el jefe was able to get the job at the dairy and la jefa got a good chamba at the nut-packing plant.

Clara's arrival coincided not only with Diana's birthday but also with the day that we moved into the new house our parents bought in a recently built neighborhood next to an orange grove. The house was not in the Mexicano section of town. But this didn't bother my parents. This was their first real home and los jefes promptly set to work to make it truly theirs. La jefa had it painted rosa Mexicana, a shocking pink, that she finished off with beige trim. To add more color, she planted rose bushes in the front. She also painted el jefe's white Ford a matte purple. El jefe thought it looked chido and redid the interior in neon-orange shag. El jefe planted fruit trees in the back and laid out a cement patio that he was too lazy to smooth down. For the next ten years of living there I was constantly scraping and cutting my knees on the textured surface of that damned patio.

That house represented my parents' Sueño Americano; but it was also the place where their relationship went to shit. El jefe would come home drunk, if he came home, because everyone knew that he was shacking up with some sucia who worked at the bar. Some nights when she waited for his possible return, la jefa would tell us stories about her life in México, Clara by her side. And the more she spent aguantando her rapidly breaking sueño Americano, the more Clara was there. We were too young to understand that feeling of abandonment, loss, and broken promises.

At least that's what I told myself later.

One night, los jefes came home frightened. They had gone out to watch a movie. *The Exorcist.* Mamá came into the house and lit candles to the Virgen de Guadalupe. Papá tried to show he was macho and not afraid by forgoing his usual beer and heading straight for the liquor cabinet. He poured himself a shot of tequila and sat silently at the bar. The next morning, when they thought we couldn't listen, we overheard la jefa telling Abuela about the movie.

¡Qué horror, Mamá! ¡Qué horror! We heard la jefa repeating over and over.

When she got to the part about the girl twisting her head 180 degrees, Diana and I turned to look down the hallway. Clara was standing there, her head tilted at an angle, her gaze firm.

Eventually we became so afraid of Clara that Diana and I decided we could no longer live under the rule of that giant. We had to get rid of her.

Our first attempt to free ourselves from Clara came when we took her out back and locked her in a toolshed. That night Diana and I both had dreams of her escaping and coming after us, her big blue eyes filled with anger. But the next day I went into the living room and there she was: Clara, silently looking at us, with her same, steady gaze. The next time we tried to abandon her we left her in the park. So as not to feel so guilty, we sat her down by the pond so she could look at the ducks. A few hours later, she was back home.

It was then that we realized that getting rid of Clara was not going to be easy.

We tried five more times to lose her.

1. We left her at the cine after a showing of *Xanadu*. We sat her down low in the aisle and simply walked away. Before getting out the door one of the attendants called la jefa to tell her that he'd found Clara hiding behind the seats.

2. We went to Silvino's for ice cream. We left her at the table and went running to el jefe's car. La jefa came out with Clara, furious at our carelessness.

3. We took her to the school playground and left her on the swings. Two hours later she was at our front door.

4. We led her into a confessional. As we were leaving misa, Antonio el Bravo, one of the altar boys, came out embarrassed as he carried her to us. Father Miguel was also pissed because la viuda García stepped into the confessional, saw Clara staring at her, and then she nearly had a heart attack.

5. On a trip to the mountains we tried to lose her in the forest. We pointed her in one direction and watched her walk away into the trees and brush. Then we ran in the opposite direction. A park ranger brought her to our car. As he put her in the seat next to a clearly frightened Diana, he said, She's so pretty, isn't she? Diana started to cry.

At night, we swore we could hear her walking through the house, pacing the halls with her slow steps. In my nightmares, I would be sitting in bed and see Clara opening the door to my room. The first times I bolted up in bed to discover that it was nothing. Later, the nightmares became more intense. I would see Clara stepping ponderously into my room. She would approach my bed, repeating my name over and over. I often woke up screaming, but later I couldn't even do that.

One night, I did wake up when I heard a sound at my door. It was Diana who came to my room to declare: Danny, we have to kill her.

Behind our house was an orange grove, and beyond that was the freeway. On summer nights Diana and I would often lay in the backyard and listen to the sounds of los traileros on their way south or north. We decided to take Clara to the freeway, thinking that a trailero would run her over or at least pick her up and take her far away.

One afternoon, we led her with great difficulty out the back gate and into the grove. As it was so hard for her to walk, we had to carry her between us. She was heavy. We looked at each other and knew we would just have to finish her off there. I remembered that el jefe kept a machete in the garage and I returned. Diana waited nervously for me with Clara. When I got back we walked her to a tree and pushed her to the ground. Diana covered her face with a one of la jefa's bandannas and we stood over her.

Clara. I still remember her arrival. She was there, standing in the doorway of our new home. Beside her was a big box that had her name painted on it in cheerful lettering: Cathy. At seven years of age with a poor command of English, I couldn't say her name, and neither could my five-year-old sister. My folks, with only a few years of living in California under their belts, couldn't pronounce her name either. They decided to call her Clara because of the color of her skin and hair. Privately, my parents called her la robot.

Clara, the four-foot-tall plastic doll. Clara, the doll that walked with outstretched arms and with a firm, unblinking blue gaze. Clara, the doll that spoke in English—Ma-ma, Ma-ma,

Ma-ma—through unmoving lips. Clara, the monster doll who entered our lives and made Diana and me accomplices in her murder.

Diana stood to one side with a small crucifix while I lifted the machete and dropped it onto Clara's arm. The thick plastic made it difficult to cut off. Clara began to kick and all we wanted to do was run. I stood on top of her until she stopped moving. After one arm I cut off the other. Then I chopped off her legs. At one point, she began to talk. I sliced at her face in fear with the machete until she stopped. After cutting her into pieces I noticed how much I was sweating. Diana helped me gather the parts and we went off into the orange grove to throw them away. A leg went into a small dump. Another ended up at the base of a tree. The arms we threw near the freeway. We buried the head and torso. We were exhausted when we got home.

Two days later, la jefa asked for Clara and we feigned ignorance. She spent a few days looking for her until she found the machete with pieces of plastic and blonde hair. We got so busted. She called us hijos del diablo and cursed us out in a long string of Spanish swear words that left us in awe of la jefa's linguistic skills. She made us kneel in the corner. I was expecting the belt. But this was far, far worse. To be sent to kneel was the absolute cruelest punishment I could think of. We had to kneel for an hour a day for an entire week while la jefa wandered around in the yard looking for the pieces of Clara.

But even with all that torture, we never fully confessed our crime.

The nightmares continued. In one, I saw Clara's different parts begin to reanimate themselves. The arms and the legs crawled toward the spot where we'd buried the torso and the head. The fingers began to dig. Once they uncovered the torso, they reattached themselves and Clara stood up. She cleaned off her dress and tried to comb her hair. Then she started to walk through the orange grove, toward our home. In my nightmare I would be standing at the window, watching the back gate as it opened. There she was, Clara, sutured together like some ragged monster.

I would wake up bathed in sweat.

For months I suffered that nightmare. In the winter, when the fog grew especially thick, I swore I saw her silhouette passing through the yard. One morning, I got up the courage to go into the grove and look for the pieces. I never found them.

By spring, the nightmares had subsided and I could finally walk around in the orange grove without feeling like I was being watched.

Years later, el jefe left for good, taking his white Mustang with him and his new family. A few months later, Diana got the cancer that hit like a meteor in the family and ended up dispersing us throughout the state. In the darkest moments while in the hospital by her side, I thought it was all Clara's revenge. But after she recovered and la jefa was able to bring us all back together I forgot about Clara.

Many years later, when my sister was living in San Francisco, I stopped to visit her on my way back to Santa Barbara. We had lunch in the Mission and afterward we stopped into Shotwell's for a drink. I told her that on my drive from Orland I passed what appeared to be doll parts by the side of the freeway.

What did you do? she asked.

What do you think? I stepped on the gas and left en chinga.

We both laughed. It was then that I told her about my nightmares of Clara. Diana stared at the walls. She changed the subject and began to tell me about her upcoming move to Istanbul.

That was the last time we mentioned Clara until one day when we were talking on the phone fifteen years later.

Soon after arriving to Dulles, I called Diana in Austin from the airport. I had just returned from Istanbul and I wanted to tell her about all of the things I'd seen in the Grand Bazaar. In particular, I wanted to tell her about this one shop full of wooden Ottoman boxes. Near the back wall there was an old porcelain doll. I shivered when I saw it.

We chatted for about twenty minutes about Clara and la jefa. La jefa had always loved dolls; she collected a lot of them. They were kept in a special glass cabinet at the end of the hallway. Often Mamá would stand Clara there. And there she would be: as if she were keeping guard, as if she wanted us to see who had her back, as if she were the leader of a doll gang. We were at this when Diana mentioned that she had to leave because she was late to meet her friend Marissa. They were going to a party out in the hill country near Austin. I promised to call the next day to talk about our plans for traveling to Turkey. She had lived in Istanbul for close to two years, and since returning more than ten years ago she had always talked about going back.

Before hanging up she told me, Sale, older brother, I'll wait for your call. We'll plan our trip to Turkey.

My flight to Albuquerque was delayed and I ended up arriving late to my house; ragged after the long flights, I left my bag on the floor and dragged myself to bed. The ringing of the telephone woke me up early. It was Marissa. She was calling from the hospital. There had been an accident. Diana had lost control of the car when they were returning from the party and ended up crashing into a tree. Marissa had been thrown from the car. She was fine, a few scratches, some bruises. But Diana, Diana. Marissa couldn't finish. Just a long pause, a deep breath, and then the crackle of white noise on the line as she thought of what to say next.

I ran out of my house with my still-unpacked bag and returned to the airport to find a flight to Texas. In the end, it wasn't the cancer that we feared would always come back to get her, it was something else.

Among Diana's things I found a number of photos from when we were kids: el jefe holding us next to the white Mustang; la jefa chasing the two of us in a park; Diana sitting on our sofa with a ball in her hands. There was a photo of her with Clara by her side. I couldn't remember when this was taken. They were holding hands, Clara towering over my sister, and Diana smiling. The photo was the only time I had ever seen my sister happy by her side.

That night, sleeping in what had been my sister's bed, I dreamed that I was walking through Sultanahmet in Istanbul, in the neighborhood between the Spice Bazaar and the Grand Bazaar. The streets were crowded as I walked past open shops, mosques, cars, and people. There was a general flow of the crowd up the hill toward the Grand Bazaar and I followed it for a while until I turned into a neighborhood of narrow streets. I was looking for the café where I knew that Diana was waiting. We were meeting to go to a party. The place was crowded and I pushed my way toward the bar. I found her.

Though the café was dark, she was sitting radiantly in a pool of light.

I thought I wasn't going to make it! I said.

She smiled and told me not to worry. She was happy to see me. I stood next to her at the bar and she asked how my trip had been. We talked awhile until I told her that I was going to step out for some air.

I'll wait for you outside so we can go to la fiesta, ok? I said.

She didn't answer, but merely smiled. It was then that I noticed a girl beside her with blonde, curly hair. I couldn't see her face because she was sitting just outside the ray of light. It was so dark.

I walked outside and started up a conversation with a couple on the street. We were talking when I saw my sister walk out of the café with the girl who had been by her side. They were both wearing veils and headscarves, which surprised me. I noticed how her friend's blonde hair slipped out from under the scarf and the weird, almost robotic way that she walked. They didn't see me, they were both deep in conversation. They were happy. They headed down the street toward the bazaar and I tried to follow. I called out to Diana but she didn't seem to hear me. She walked rapidly with her blonde friend. I knew then that I was not going to catch up.

I just watched them walk farther and farther away.

Walking Spanish

SOMETIMES I WOULD WAKE up in the middle of the night and think about those people who, for whatever reason, had dropped out of my life. Those who had, for a time, purified my mind, made everything fall into place, changed—like the song says—all the lead sleeping in my head into gold. Whatever happened to them? Looking up at the ceiling of the rented flat, with the double-paned windows shut to cut out most of the noise and the heavy black curtains in place—because night in Madrid cannot be fully contained, a friend once told me—I would think about those friends and lovers, lost in my memory.

And I'm out and about in Madrid, walking the streets of La Latina, Lavapies, Opera, checking out the sights and sounds of that hot, hot July. I've found me a cheap flat down near Puerta de Toledo, near the Rastro. Walking Spanish down the street, with my iPod on and listening to a mix of the Decemberists, *Rain Dogs*–era Tom Waits, Arcade Fire, and Radio Tarifa. It is summer in Madrid and at two in the afternoon the city slumbers along as people head out for lunch and the shops close for siesta.

Madrid is a city where you'll find more people on the street at 3 a.m. than at 3 p.m., a friend told me years ago while we were working in a tiny electronics-repair shop in Chico. I had come back to Northern California after finishing my degree at Dartmouth. As I pondered where to go next, I moved home and found a job in Chico, twenty miles from Orland. The electronics shop needed someone to work out in front, answering phones, receiving items to be repaired, tracking orders. It was an easy job for the summer. It was one of the technicians who had made the comment about Madrid; he had been living there off and on for a few years before settling down in Northern California.

A couple of years later, after graduating with a master's in geography, I made my first trip to Madrid. I got a teaching gig at some instituto, teaching English to businessmen and business students hoping to land a job with a multinational corporation. I taught at various sites; my favorite was a meeting room in the Torre Picasso, a skyscraper designed by the same architect who did the former World Trade Center in New York. Before class I often stood at the window of the meeting room on the forty-second floor and looked out over the Castellana toward Bernabéu stadium.

In truth, thinking about the Torre Picasso now kind of scares me. Mostly because it looks like a stubby version of one of the twin towers.

I spent a year living in Madrid, walking the streets and teaching English in random office buildings throughout the city. After a few months, I thought that I would never return to the United States. I was going to become an expat and do expat things. That's what I had planned. On the overnight train to Barcelona, I met a fellow expat in the bar car. She was living in Barcelona. We talked about the differences between the two cities. I told her that a friend had said that Madrid was the perfect city if you were single, and that Barcelona was more for couples. She seemed to agree, and told me that's what she liked about Barcelona, as she was rarely single. Basically, she told me, I'm just hoeing around. And then she laughed. We continued talking through the night about how we were basically set in Spain and there was no reason to return. In the morning we went our separate ways and I never saw her again.

Eventually I did return, but then I spent the next few years bouncing back and forth between Madrid, New York—when I was doing my graduate work—and San Francisco. But then my visits became infrequent, and soon I stopped going altogether—primarily because I was married—until I got an offer from the Complutense to be a visiting professor for a year.

One night I'm with friends in a bar down the street from the Plaza de Santo Domingo. We had started off with dinner at a Japanese restaurant around the corner, then moved up to a Galician bar for cañas before heading to the next corner to an Asturian place. We were celebrating Gabi, who had just won a literary award.

And then I see her.

Almost a decade later, I run into Catalina again. The Peruvian journalist with streaked light-brown hair, with a vaguely hippie-ish air, the one I spent a few years flirting back and forth with as we moved through various other relationships. She is there at a nearby table with friends. Her hair is darker, longer, she's wearing a black dress, her glasses are black. She sees me and for an instant doesn't recognize me.

Then it happens, the awareness spreading across her face.

I first met her at a party over on Hortaleza. It was a warm night and I stepped out onto the balcony to watch the crowds lining up to get into the bar next door. Soon, this pretty woman in a black-and-white cocktail dress came out to the balcony for a smoke. We didn't talk for a long while. Finally she looked at me and asked: What's the weirdest thing you've done while drunk? I looked at her. She was wearing a blue wig and in her hand she held a cigarette and a cocktail.

You first, I responded.

I don't know, she said, taking a drink, and then she leaned forward. But I'll tell you in six months.

I leaned back and was about to laugh when she shrugged and walked back inside the apartment.

Two months later, I was in New York City and starting a PhD program. The following summer I returned to Madrid. One night, while walking back from the Plaza Dos de Mayo, I ran into her on the street. She looked at me and asked, Well?

Well? I responded.

What's the weirdest thing you've ever done while drunk?

I applied for a doctoral program and got in.

She arched an eyebrow. Not bad, she finally said.

And you?

I stole a camel from a zoo.

We spent most of the summer together, often shrugging off our respective partners so that we could run off to the movies or just walk around. It was something we often did whenever I flew to Spain.

Another night out with friends, I ended up at El Jardín Secreto. She was there, at the bar with another group of friends. When I approached to order, she called out to the bartender, He'll have a caipirinha.

Then she explained to me, You will, because it's OUR drink.

She didn't talk to me the rest of the night, though I noticed that she would often glance over to our group.

This other night after a concert, my Cosa at the time suggested we go somewhere for a drink. I suggested we head over to Bar Susan, but she didn't want to walk so far, so she suggested we go to El Jardín Secreto. At a table near the window I saw Catalina with her Cosa. We pretended not to notice each other, but when I headed over to the bathroom she was soon behind me. So, she whispered, how's your Caos?

When the server came to take our orders, my Cosa ordered a gin and tonic and I ordered a caipirinha. I could feel Catalina's eyes burning a hole through me.

For years I had imagined running into her again and pretending that I didn't know her, acting as if my good-bye all those years ago had been final and that she had ultimately disappeared into my past. Acting as if she were someone I simply used to know. But now with her there, I realize that I can't hide the emotions.

But we pretend that they don't exist. We hug and talk to each other, haltingly at first. We update the other on what we've been doing. She came back to Madrid about five years ago; she works for a small independent record company. When I knew her she was a journalist, but now she is a lawyer. We talk some more. Then it's time to leave and we both head out together. We walk to metro Opera. She's headed up to Rubén Darío, I'm headed down to Puerta de Toledo.

And there we are, on the train platform, on opposite sides. We talk across the divide. Just before her train arrives she tells me it was good to see me again. Then the train pulls in and she gets on. I stand on the platform, watching her train pull away.

We never spoke about meeting again.

Days without Paracetamol

THE END OF DECEMBER and here we are in Chicago, the Outer Territories of Aztlán. Ha. A cold day. A fucking cold day. From the window of this room I see a frozen river covered in ice. Down below. Twenty-two stories. Fuck. That's a drop. There are people down there, walking along Michigan Avenue, heading toward the Million Dollar Avenue to do some shopping on a frigid day at the end of the year. It's gray outside. The sky is steel. The people down below try to hide from the cold, but they're determined to do their shopping. Off in the distance, I can see columns of steam rising from a few of the buildings on the other side of the river.

I would prefer not to see any of this. It makes me cold.

But then, I wanted a room with a view, right?

I'm going to tell you a story about something that happened a long time ago. Back when I was an undergrad at Chico State, over in Northern California. I'm going to tell you about the time I last saw my father. It was over in the mall, North Valley Plaza, what we all called "the old mall." It was around this time, the end of the year. I had stopped thinking about him. I only remembered him as a few loose memories, blurry photos kept in a box, some comments of his that a tío or a tía would bring up every so often, usually at family reunions.

North Valley Plaza. As a mall it was a bit of a joke. But as a kid, it was the place to go. It was our weekly ritual. The folks would pile us all into the car and off to Chico we would go. Sometimes, after the mall we would go to the cine, since back then our local movie theater in Orland didn't show any Mexican films for our local community of farm and field workers. No, that would come later. So back then, the entertainment for the Mexicano community was in Chico, at that small movie theater. It's no longer there. It was torn down years ago and converted into a parking lot. But in its day, that cine was ground zero for the Mexicanos. Before the movie, they would play these newsreels that showed what was happening in Mexico. There was also a presenter who would come out and have these contests before the newsreels and also during intermission. My sister and I would run up and down the aisles of the packed theater. One time we even managed to make it onstage during the movie and our giant shadows were projected on the screen.

Afterward we would have dinner and then Papá would drive home while my siblings and I would sleep after the long day at the mall and then the cine. The mall. We would spend a long time there. I remember the time we went to Montgomery Ward to look at paint. Mamá and Papá had bought a house and la jefa was decorating it. She showed me a pale eggshell blue and asked me if I liked it for my room. Back then my favorite color was red, but at the age of six I knew that red was not the color for a boy. I went with the pale blue. For my sister's room she chose a pale pink. To this day I can't stand pale blue and if my sister were still alive I know she would continue to hate pink.

Of course, all this was before the Event. The Cataclysm. The divorce of my jefes and the cancer of my sister.

After it all went down I started having headaches. They weren't migraines, not completely. But they hurt. I never told anyone how much. With all that I saw at the hospital or at home—Mamá crying over the mounting hospital bills, the pleading by my brother and sister to be allowed to come live with us again, her sobbing at night when she thought I was asleep—I thought that my headaches were nothing to complain about.

That was also about the time I started to close myself off. I tried to make myself hard. Harder than stone, harder than steel. Nothing would affect me. Not even Kryptonite. With everything that was happening at home and at the hospital, I couldn't process it all. I no longer wanted to deal with all that. My system was on overload. I no longer wanted to feel. The only thing I thought I could do was kill it all, bury my emotions in a trunk at the bottom of the sea. I had to make myself numb to everything. Cover my heart in rubber so tough that everything would bounce off.

Life can sometimes lead us to the most drastic solutions.

The divorce, followed by the cancer of my younger sister, cost my jefa a lot. She had to make the most drastic of choices: she had to send us all away so that she could dedicate herself to my sister.

Maybe if my pops hadn't sold the house, kicking us out onto the street, maybe we could've all lived together. Of course, he determined the terms of the divorce. He told her, You can keep the kids. But I keep everything else. And if you want anything more than that, I'm taking the kids too.

My jefa, she had no idea what to do. She had followed this man eight hundred miles north of the border, taking her from her family and the comfort she knew to a rural farming community in Northern California. She had yet to become the fierce, strong woman I later knew. Back then she was scared of losing us.

She accepted the shitty offer.

With no house, a sick daughter, and a lack of money, she had to make the decision to send us to live with different relatives. My brother and my youngest sister went to live with a tía in Orland where we lived. My sister went to Stanford. I was the last one to find a home. It was as if I was cursed by my dad's mother when she stood up at a party, pointed a finger at me, and declared: This is all your fault. Then she sat down and did not say another word until the party ended. As the oldest son, I knew what she meant: I ruined my father by being born.

My uncles in Orland didn't want me with them. What could they do with a cursed nephew? No, it was better to send the marked boy to another place, another family.

Far.

Far away, so that the curse wouldn't crash down upon them.

My other relatives turned their backs, claiming that they already had too many children to care for, or, in one particular case, they simply said no.

I ended up living with some distant relatives in San Diego. They accepted because my jefa promised to pay them.

What a fucking tragedy the whole thing was.

Moms found a job in a chip-making plant in Silicon Valley so that she could be near my sister who was in the Children's Hospital at Stanford. Before moving south, I lived with her in an apartment in Mountain View. Across the street was the middle school I attended for a semester. It seemed perfect. However, the apartment complex where we lived didn't accept children. The apartment manager made an exception for my sister because she was going to spend most of her time in the hospital. Since I had no other place to go I had to live clandestinely.

For four months I would sneak out of the apartment in the morning to go to school. Afterward, I had to go straight home and lock myself inside with the curtains drawn. I could not make any noise, and if I wanted to watch TV, I had to keep the volume down, extremely low. Moms worked until late and then she would go to the hospital. She would come home at night and make dinner. The two of us would eat in silence at the table. When my sister was not in the hospital things were a little better. The three of us would have dinner and afterward la jefa would draw us in close and say, This is how it was in the beginning, just the three of us.

But when my sister wasn't there, it was just me in the apartment until Moms came home. I would spend the afternoons reading comic books or writing stories in my notebooks. In some I was an explorer looking for a hidden treasure in the mountains. In a few I was a Jedi fighting against the evil empire. In others I was a secret agent in battle against a malevolent organization.

In the majority of my stories, I was a prisoner locked in a tower on a small island in the ocean. I was guarded by an ogre, and in each of my adventures I would try to send a message to my sister who was also imprisoned in another tower far from me.

Sometimes at school, I had a session with Mrs. Parsons, the school psychologist. She would pull out photos and ask me to tell her what was happening in each. I liked that. Telling stories.

She showed me a photo of some kids sitting around a table. There was a smiling mom about to serve dinner. Mrs. Parsons asked me about the father, who was not present at the table. I said that he was on a business trip and that he was happy because he knew his family was safe and together. I never told her what I really thought: that el jefe wasn't there because he was at the bar with his friends and his novia. The kids and the mom were happy because el jefe wasn't there to yell or to hit la jefa.

I remember a night when el jefe came home drunk and sent us all to our rooms. Then he leapt at my jefa with one of my youngest sister's toys. My sister ran from her room to stop him. I stayed in my room with my brother, holding him tight and singing a song. My youngest sister was crying in her crib. When he was finished, el jefe looked at me and smiled before he left the house. This was your fault, his look told me. I went to my jefa's room and saw a long dark stain of blood on the wall. She was lying on the floor.

I helped my moms call the police for the last time. Then, I walked outside with the bloody toy and headed for my bike.

On the weekends, I would stay in the hospital with my sister. The nurses were really nice and they set up a cot for me right next to her. The rooms were for six kids. The second time I stayed there, I met Trina's parents; she was a three-year-old with leukemia. Henry was in another bed. He was a fourteen-year-old with hemophilia. There was also Lisa, another girl with leukemia. She was eleven, like my sister. They later became great friends. Tim was the son of an astronaut and he had a rare form of cancer. He spent a lot of time in the Experimental Medicine section of the hospital. Finally there was Juliet; she was operated on the same week as my sister. She also had her leg amputated. She had long hair and it had started to fall out. There were a few nights in which I heard her crying for her lost hair.

And despite all that sadness—the children who would die at night or who would simply be moved out to never return, the medicines that would leave her exhausted and without strength to raise her arm, the constant blood samples being taken—my sister always remained positive, especially around my moms. But I could tell she was terrified. At night, she would ask me to tell her stories. At first, I would recount comic books I had just read or what I saw on TV. But later, I began to tell her the stories I made up in the apartment. I told her about secret messages in bottles thrown from towers in the hope that they would arrive safely, about battles on other planets, about quests with elves and dwarves to save a dying town. She would often fall asleep before I finished. I would then lie down on my cot and listen to the machines that were connected to the other kids and the sounds of the hospital at night.

When the headaches came, I would hold out as much as I could. I didn't want to complain. I would lie on the cot and cover my head with the pillow. Joy, one of the nurses, noticed I was in pain and she began to give me acetaminophen. Often, after taking the pills, I would lie on the bed next to my sister and stare out the window. I felt how my headache would diminish as the pain flowed outside my body. Years later, when I was living in Spain, I discovered that acetaminophen was called paracetamol over there. I liked that name. Paracetamol. Paracetamol for the pain. Paracetamol for the cure.

After six months, my clandestine life was too much. My attempts at achieving invisibility were failing. The apartment manager caught me a couple of times and my jefa was running out of excuses for my presence. At Christmas, she was able to convince a distant cousin to let me live with her and her family in San Diego.

I didn't want to leave my sister, but there was nothing I could do. I lived for a year with that family until my moms was able to have my sister moved to a hospital in San Diego. A few months later, she was able to have my younger brother and sister move back with us, and almost two years after having to separate us, our jefa was able to bring us all back together under the same roof.

The next year, with my sister's cancer now in remission, we moved again: back to Orland where we had grown up. Even though our jefa's family was from the border, and most of my jefe's family lived up north, Moms still felt a connection to that town. So we ended up returning to the place where it all began, and those three years that we spent wandering become a parentheses in our lives. A blip. One of those moments that we all tried to forget.

I don't know why I'm telling you all this. Context maybe. Maybe it's because we're in this hotel room high above Michigan Avenue. Maybe it's because I feel like confessing. Maybe it's because my ex-wife used to always complain that I never talked, that I always came off as distant.

By the time I was in college, the mall was in clear decline. A lot of stores closed down after the new mall was built on the other side of town. Despite all that, I would still go out there when I moved to Chico. It was part of my past, I guess. Since I didn't have a car, I would ride my bike. I would park it near the Montgomery Ward and my walk would begin there. It wasn't until a long time later that I realized that I was following the same route as my parents. We would begin in Ward's and then would walk into the mall to go to the other stores.

However, I rarely went into the stores. I would just walk. In moments of stress or boredom, I would head out there. I had this friend in one of my classes—this awesome anthropology class that always blew us away—Daniel, or tocayo as I called him, who thought I was nuts for my mall trips. He didn't get it. I don't think I did either. But I would go out there and somehow the mall with its empty shops and few people would calm me. This certainly didn't happen in other malls; they've always made me nervous. But that one, I don't know, it calmed me. Especially on those days when I would ride out there and I would suddenly get a headache and I would find myself without paracetamol.

It was a day like today. The day I saw my jefe at the mall. He was out in front of the Hickory Farms, that place that sells cheese and smoked sausages. He was there in front of the sausage. My dad. I hadn't seen him in six years. Not since that day, months after that bloody night, when he drove over to watch us move out of the house. He was coming out not to say good-bye but to make sure that Moms didn't take anything more than was discussed in the terms of the divorce. He didn't talk to us, only to Moms.

Before he left, he looked at her and then at us. One day I'll see you living on the street with those dirty kids of yours. And on that day, I'll be happy, he told her with a smile.

Then he drove away in his recently repaired Mustang.

I wanted to throw a rock at it. But the bravery that I felt that night was gone: I was back to my shy, timid self.

I thought about avoiding him. Just walking past and moving on, and I was going to do that until I found myself stopping and saying, Hi, Dad.

Without surprise he turned around and stared at me for a few seconds. What are you doing here? he finally asked.

Typical of him.

When he spoke to me in English I wasn't surprised. Ever since I had been five he had spoken like that. I looked at him and answered in Spanish: Nada.

Good. That's good, he responded, and then he started looking at the sausages.

He was like that for a while, not saying a word and keeping his back to me. He expected me to just walk away. Our meeting was over.

I stood there, even though my head had started to hurt. There was a pharmacy nearby and I knew I could get something for the pain, but I decided to remain. I wanted to see what he would do.

Finally, he sighed deeply. He invited me to sit at some nearby benches. As soon as he sat, he started to complain about work and about his bosses. He didn't care if I knew who he was talking about or not. His was simply a litany of complaints.

Moms once told me that in the beginning el jefe would come home from work and just start complaining. If he felt that he was being passed over for anything—if a coworker got a raise, if someone reproached him, if he heard a comment he perceived as racist—he would complain and complain, as if expecting that my jefa could solve everything.

Some say I should have been the one who got the cancer. Since I was the one who ruined my father, the curse should have fallen on me. But it didn't. Not really. My sister lost her leg; I got the guilt.

Seeing my father in the mall wasn't that great showdown that one would think. We sat down on a bench in front of Hickory Farms and he complained about work, about all the hours, and about his bosses. They were complaints that you would make to anyone you met on the street. He finally asked what I was up to. I responded that I was almost finishing up my studies at the university.

He stared at me with a look of mild disgust. Why are you wasting your time? he finally said.

And then he continued, Ponte a trabajar.

After leaving the house, I had found el jefe in his favorite bar. Of course. He headed straight there. I stood outside, not knowing what to do. I didn't want to go inside. I knew that I did not want to ever be like my father. I felt that if I walked in there, it would be my first step into becoming him.

The Mustang was parked in front. I threw myself at it. With a rock I scratched the paint, then I found a larger rock and broke the windshield. I threw the bloody toy into the front seat and walked away. There were sirens in the distance. I hopped on my bike and rode home.

We didn't talk about the past. He didn't ask about the family, Moms, my siblings. I wanted to tell him that my sister was doing well, that she had beat the cancer and was now living in Austin. It seemed as if that curse that had fallen onto my family had passed, that we were on the other side, survivors.

None of this came up. He didn't even say anything about the car. His daughter arrived and looked at me for a long time.

I know you. You're my brother, she said.

Then she took my dad's hand. We said good-bye without affection. The two of them started walking toward the exit. I noted that my father limped a little. He had gotten old.

Lupe and the Stars

TODD WAS THE BOYFRIEND of my best friend, Lupe. As kids we three were a band of outsiders. He was our leader. He was the class bookworm: he read comics whenever he could, but later exchanged those for books by Stephen King, and in high school he reached for novels by Kurt Vonnegut. At times he was Spider-Man, Kalimán, Captain Nemo, the Invisible Man, a Jedi warrior, a musketeer at the service of a prince imprisoned by an evil aunt, an astronaut on an intergalactic journey. He was also a traveler lost in time, trapped in a year and a place where he did not belong. He was the boy who at thirteen had to suddenly become the man of the house when our father abandoned us.

He was all of these things to me. But when he became a cholo and later a junkie, that was when my older brother Todd crossed the line.

Becoming a tecato was too much. And it didn't help that Lupe followed along.

Lupe. She is sitting beside me. She doesn't say a word. We're on the old Sutliff Bridge over the Cedar River. She looks up. At the night. At the stars.

These Iowan nights remind me of our childhood in California, she tells me after a while.

We've known each other since we were kids, morros running around the olive orchards and the orange groves of our Northern Californian town. When we were twelve, Lupe and I would run between the trees to find a place to rest and read the latest from the Fantastic Four, Batman, Kalimán, or our personal favorite, Green Lantern. Todd would be over at another tree reading Stephen King.

A few years earlier, Todd often joined us in our games and adventures. In one of my favorites, I got to play the hero, the role he usually played. In this game I would be a member of the Green Lantern Corps and with my green ring I would become a super-hero. I would hear a cry for help and run out into the orchard where I would raise my ring and shout out the Green Lantern pledge: "In brightest day, in blackest night, no evil shall escape my sight . . ." Then I would go off to help my friends: Todd, in his role as an astronaut battling an alien from Planet X; Lupe, as a reporter in danger from a giant bee mutated because of the pesticides used on the fields; a family—Todd and Lupe—escaping from "Toro" Fernández, a bad kid who we imagined could control zombies, demons, and the migra.

Years later, when I watched how I was losing them both, I imagined that in some hidden place I could find my green ring of power and with that I could save them. But by then, I knew it was too late.

When she was fifteen, Lupe began to hear the call of the cholas. And that—as I already knew with the example of Adela—was a strong call. We would sit on the hill in the children's park and I could tell she was losing interest in the comic books and our fantasies. I noted how she was paying more attention to the cholas sitting at the entrance to the park. Beside them were the cholos leaning against their carefully detailed cars. It was obvious they were much more interesting than comic-book superheroes since their costumes didn't consist of capes or tights. They wore loose-fitting clothing: extra-large ironed white T-shirts and pressed khakis. The cholas wore their hair up high and held in place by hair spray; the cholos had short hair and bandannas wrapped around their foreheads. Instead of names like Wonder Woman, Ant Man, Supergirl, or Batman, they had better names like La Sleepy, El Tróbel, La Mousie, Sir Muecas, Giggles, Lil Puppet, Leidi Baga. Shit like that.

I knew that I lost Lupe the day I went to the children's park and found her sitting with the cholas. She saw me head into the park carrying my comic books but she didn't call out my name. She knew I wasn't interested in becoming a cholo. Soon after I heard them start to call her Shy Girl.

From then on, I saw her less until she started going out with Todd. After his first year at Cornell, he returned home dressed like a cholo. Dreamer, they started to call him.

When he looked at chola Lupe, she looked back at him. The Dreamer and the Shy Girl.

There's this photo in one of our family albums. I think it's the only picture of the two of them, since after what happened to Todd, Moms dumped all the blame on Lupe and went so far as to prohibit mentioning her at home. In the photo, Todd and Lupe are walking through the park holding hands. He wears pressed khaki pants with a white T-shirt and thin black suspenders. Lupe wears black pants and a tank top. Her hair is carefully combed high on her head and she's sporting green eye shadow. The two simply shine, and I remember how everyone just stopped to admire them as they walked through the park. It was late afternoon and a golden glow illuminated the two of them and amplified their joy. They look blessed. They really do. Together in the photo they walk in the aura of their joy, certain that no one or anyone can take them from their bliss.

Lupe. I hadn't seen her in more than ten years. One afternoon, after teaching my seminar, I found her sitting in front of my office on campus. A beat-up suitcase by her side. I almost didn't recognize her.

Hey, Punk Rocker, she said and smiled.

Hey, Shy Girl, I responded.

She lowered her head and her black hair fell over her face.

It's been years since anyone called me that.

Same here.

On the road from Iowa City to West Liberty, I told her I was happy she went to look for me on campus, especially since I had moved about six months earlier. I bought a house in West Liberty, a small town about fifteen miles away. I liked it because it was small and because it had a large Mexicano population.

Sounds like Orland, she responded.

You'll see.

Before arriving to the house I drove her around town. We passed through downtown and I showed her the old buildings and the one movie theater. We drove past the meat-packing plant and I told her that it reminded me of the Musco olive plant that used to be in Orland. I pointed out how instead of being surrounded by orange groves and olive orchards, my new town ended in cornfields. Lupe was speechless. Finally, she said I was loco for leaving California to end up living in the Iowan version of our hometown.

My house is close to downtown, I explained to her. It has some large windows, but it doesn't have a yard. If it looks like a store, it's because it used to be. The ex-owners bought an old general store and converted it into a house. They lived there for about ten years until I bought it from them.

We definitely don't have this in Orland, she responded with surprise when we pulled up to the house.

Later, after fixing up a space for her in my spare room, I went to sit outside while Lupe rested. I watched the cars pass and I thought of the last time I saw her.

It was the fifth anniversary of Todd's death, and I returned to

Orland to be with my family. I was living in San Diego then, working on my doctorate, and at first I didn't want to go so as not to miss classes. It was my sister who convinced me.

Eddie, we need to be together to support Mamá. I don't know why, but this year has been really hard for her. I hopped on a Greyhound and headed north.

That first night, I decided to go for a walk through town. Heading out into the cool night, I thought about the geography of migration class that I was taking. I thought of how my own family was marked by migration. My parents crossed the border a few months before Todd was born. They crossed because my dad had some uncles here and they told him he could get a good job at Musco. They arrived, as Moms told me years later, in a Greyhound bus from the border. They came with little: three suitcases and nothing more. A year after Todd was born, my moms—pregnant with me—returned to Mexico with a suitcase, a child in diapers, and another on the way. She also had the intention to never return across the line. In El Norte, my pops could keep doing what he wanted on his own: getting drunk in the bars and then coming home with anger in his eyes. He could beat someone else up. That's what Moms thought. She had put up with it, the beatings and the drunken anger, until the night he came home and angrily kicked Todd's crib. The next day, she packed her stuff and left. It was her father who returned us to El Norte. He took us home and then waited in the kitchen. When Dad came home, he sat my father down and admonished him to never beat on his wife or family again. The threats must have worked because Pops didn't touch Moms for years. Then Abuelo died. And Pops got his revenge.

Moms told me all this a week after Todd was buried. My siblings were inside the house and Moms and I were out on the porch. We looked at the towers of the Musco plant, now closed because the company moved the plant to Tracy. Inside, I had my bag packed and I was ready to return to New Hampshire. I knew that Moms didn't want me to leave. At the same time, she knew that it was something I had to do. The word had already spread that, for us, the children of Mexican farmworkers, our destiny was to not go far away. The story of Todd demonstrated that the Ivy League was not for us; our lot was to stay close to home.

And that's what happened. My cousin Daniel went off to Chico State, twenty miles from Orland. Hugo also. Giggles, after a lot of fights with her dad, who didn't want her to study, was able to convince him to let her take classes at the community college. After a few years she went off to Sacramento State and became an engineer. Beto Fernández went to San José. Fidencio went further, to San Luis Obispo. He took the Tapia twins, Manuel and Samuel, with him. And after their years of study, many of them returned to Orland and its neighboring towns.

Lupe though. Lupe didn't leave. She stayed.

As I walked through the streets that night, five years after Todd's death, I thought about all those moments with my brother and Lupe after he returned from Cornell. I walked past the building where Lupe crashed after her father kicked her out. He ran her off when he caught her high on something. She ended up renting a cheap apartment that she occasionally shared with Todd. After two years away he came back different. From the promising nerd star of his class he became the stereotype of the brown gangster everyone at Cornell expected him to be: the worst grades, multiple absences, and many problems with the administration. He was also arrested for holding up gas stations between Ithaca and Syracuse. I remember the phone calls and my moms having to find a bail bondsman to get that knucklehead out of jail. Before he could be kicked out of the university for good he packed his bags and returned to Califas.

He came back skinnier, distant, and nervous. I could see in his eyes that he was fighting with addiction.

Todd returned the night of my high school graduation. I was accepted to Dartmouth and Moms was adamant that I was not going to accept. But it was Todd who convinced her. Even though the shithead was always getting into trouble, she never stopped believing in him. She denied everything that we saw. His change in style, his nervousness, the strange pauses in his conversation. The distant stare. Moms denied it all. She would respond: he's always been quiet, he's always been a loner, he's always been living in his own special world.

From the kid who was creative and introspective, he was now much more closed off. As a kid, he used to love to draw and he would talk about growing up to become an artist or a comic-book writer. Now, he was simply mostly in a daze. Many times he couldn't even follow a conversation. He would leap from topic to topic. Other times he would suddenly stop. Just stop.

I guess that's why his cholo friends decided to call him Dreamer.

But for me, he was always Todd.

On my walk past the high school, I stopped for a while at the football field. I sat on the bleachers and stared out over the field where we had our graduation ceremonies. I remembered my graduation, seven years before. After the ceremony, Todd was one of the first to congratulate me. He came bounding through the crowd to embrace me in a strong hug. I could tell that he had been out in the parking lot with his boys, the other cholos. Before he left for Cornell they saw him as a nerd or a coconut who had rejected his own raza to be white. When he returned to Orland in his cholo style, after his first year away, they accepted him as one of their own.

Carnalito, mi carnalito, you did it, ése, you did it, he said as he spun me around and hugged me. I'm so proud of you, ése. Mi carnalito, no sabes lo proud that I am of you, cabrón.

And to congratulate me, he gave me a small bag of weed.

It's weak, ése, I got something a little more, you know, potente over there with los homeboys. But you, my brother, you should not even partake of that. He told me with a grin.

I smiled back and put the bag in my pocket. Later that night, I threw it out. After he saw me he headed straight for Lupe, who had barely graduated. It was through my help that she was able to pass. They both headed off to continue partying with their homies.

I didn't see my brother for another three days.

The summer before I left for New Hampshire, Todd and I shared a room again. At first it was a lot of fun because he would spend the nights talking about his life on the East Coast. He told me about the whacked shit he saw, from the usual racism of the privileged white elite to the surprising racism from the "Hispanics" who came from families with money. Because he was the bato who came out of the fields, everyone expected him to confirm their own ideas: that he was just another underprivileged kid who should accept the benevolence of the obvious affirmative action that got him into Cornell—so stay in your place, son—and be an example of the impoverished, oppressed minority. Those who had never experienced racism expected Todd to be a symbol of it so that they could affirm that they knew what marginality and poverty felt like. And, after a few months, that is exactly what he did. I could imagine it perfectly, the boy astronaut taking off his space helmet to tie a bandanna around his neck and put on some baggy khakis and an extra-large shirt; it was just another role in a life of roles.

Todd, the boy nerd who dreamed of being an astronaut; now Dreamer, the cholo.

Lupe spent a lot of time at home with us. At first, she would arrive after dinner and the two would head off to the bedroom. I would stay planted on the couch because Todd would give me a Don't Come Around look. After a few hours, she would leave and he would sit down on the couch with me.

What's on? he would ask.

Nothing, I would always respond.

Later, he started bringing her around at night. He would leave the window open and she would sneak in around midnight. I would be trying to sleep in my bed but I could hear the two of them fumbling around under the covers. Sometimes, I would wake up to see them seated at the window, passing a joint. Todd without a shirt and Lupe in her panties, smoking by the light of the moon.

I never told Moms anything. But I'm sure she knew. Mexican moms are like that. Psychic and shit. Nothing would escape her. But she wouldn't say anything either. What she did was to convert the garage into a room for Todd. By then, he was spending more time at Lupe's place and so I would hang out in the garage reading his old comic books. A year after I started at Dartmouth, Todd went off to live in San Francisco with some friends. A few months after that, he was living on the streets.

One night, when we were still sharing a room, I heard Todd tell Lupe that what he liked most about her was her hair. He said he loved to run his hands through it, get lost in it. Then he covered his face with it and began to moan. She called him loco, laughed, and rolled away.

After leaving the high school, I headed for the park that was across the street. The children's park was there and I remembered the night that I watched *Close Encounters of the Third Kind* at home. Todd had sent it to me from Cornell. It was one of his favorite movies and when it came out on videotape he scooped it up, probably literally, from a video store. After seeing it, I went out for a walk and ended up in the children's park where we had all played as kids. I headed for the hill that was in the center. Beneath it was a series of tunnels where we used to hide out. Sometimes Todd and I pretended to be soldiers looking for the enemy base at the bottom of a volcano. Other times, we imagined ourselves stranded astronauts on a strange planet like in *Robinson Crusoe on Mars* or in *Lost in Space*. There were times when Lupe would join us in our adventures. After reading the comic-book version of *The Time Machine*, Todd made us pretend we were all time travelers lost in an age that was not our own. Always, after running around the park and through the tunnels, we would end up lying on the top of the hill, staring at the sky.

When we were older, we still liked to go there to sit and tell stories. After the movie, I rode my bike to the park, my head full of UFOs and aliens. I lay on the hill and watched the stars. I was trying to figure out which of them could be a spaceship when Lupe brought me out of my searching.

Lalo, what's up? She looked at me and sat down by my side. She was in her chola look, but it was still new to her and she was unsure of whether she liked it. She was wearing baggy pants and a tank top. I was wearing a T-shirt that one of my cousins from Los Angeles had sent me. It was for a punk band, the Zeros. My cousin was big into punk and he sent me T-shirts and tapes of bands like the Zeros, the Bags, X, and the Plugz. I often shared the stuff with my cousin Daniel who had returned to Orland after a couple of years of drifting around California while his sister was in the hospital.

I see that you and me are changing our looks, she told me. I'm going to start calling you Punk Rocker.

I laughed and said, Good name. And yeah, I guess we are changing. Soon we won't even recognize each other.

We sat there a long time. Finally, she said that her friends wanted to give her a new name. Something for the gang. They wanted to call her Sad Eyes. I thought that was fucking dramatic. I looked at how her hair covered half her face.

Why not Shy Girl? I suggested.

She thought about it a while. La Shy Girl, she said to herself. Then she looked up at the stars. That doesn't sound bad. I like it.

We sat there not saying anything. Then she stood up, looked me directly in the eye, and walked away. I returned to watching the stars and thinking about spaceships.

As I walked through the park I remembered the funeral. A lot of people showed up. Many came out of respect for my moms. Others came for the chisme. My tías, the ones who often turned a blind eye to us—especially when Moms needed money—came crying over the death of Todd. His schoolteachers came to pay their respects. I watched the passing people and thought about what Todd had told me once. People always expect you to confirm whatever fucked up idea they have about you. For some, my brother was the typical tecato who got the death he deserved; for others he was the star child who got lost; for his gang he was the homie felled in battle; for my moms, he was the oldest son whose job it was to raise us all out of the depths after the divorce and who got lost in the attempt.

The only person who wasn't there was Lupe. I later found out it was because Moms declared that she could not be there. Moms claimed that it was all her fault Todd had gotten lost. Lupe had to say good-bye to my brother in private. Years later, she told me that she didn't really care: she was tweaking so hard before the funeral. She claimed she needed it because she felt that Todd was by her side. He was leading her through the fog of all that was happening.

The moon was full and large when I got to the children's park that night. I saw her there. Lupe, sitting on top of the hill. I hadn't seen her since before the funeral. She was looking up at the stars. I stayed there awhile, standing under a tree. I left without calling her and walked back home. A few days later I took the bus back to San Diego without having talked to her.

I didn't see her again until that afternoon in November when I found her at my office. Through friends I knew that since Todd's death she had become more of a junkie, that she didn't hit bottom until she ended up like him, living on the streets of San Francisco. That night out on the Sutliff Bridge she told me that she woke up one morning in an alley near City Hall and she realized that she could no longer live like that. She needed help. She walked out of the alley and headed home. It took her a long time to recover and become clean.

She got my address from one of my sisters. They ran into each other out in front of Big John's Market and they started to talk. They talked a long time until Lupe got the strength to ask for my address. A few weeks later she hopped on a Greyhound bus headed east.

A few days after arriving, she told me that the trip from California had taken her almost a week and that every time she had a long layover or she had to change buses—in Sacramento, Reno, Salt Lake City, Denver, and Omaha—she doubted whether to continue or not to Iowa City. She was unsure whether I would let her into my house or whether it was a good idea to see me.

I was happy to see her, though I didn't really know what to think of her surprise visit. It had been a long time since I had thought of her or of Todd. My brother didn't visit me in dreams as often anymore. I rarely thought of our final conversation when he called me from San Francisco. The connection had been awful and full of white noise. His voice, already a whisper, coming in through all of that was haunting. I could feel the distance in it, in his odd pauses and his words that would end in whispers. It sounded as if he was calling me from Mars or from another planet. For many years, I would wake up in the early morning and hear that sound, that white noise, that signal that seemed to be coming from somewhere far, far away.

In the days that we were together, Lupe told me about her life in the previous years, about her attempts at winding that string of her life that she felt had become unwound. She also spoke of our childhood when we would run through the orchards and the fields, of the afternoons when we would lie on a hill to read comics or to look up at the sky. She never mentioned Todd though, even though I always felt that his presence was between us. It wasn't until that night when we were sitting on the Sutliff Bridge that he came up.

Sitting on the bridge with the Cedar River flowing beneath us in the dark, she began to tell me about that morning when she woke up in the alley.

You're not going to believe me, she tells me. I saw Todd that morning. Neta. Truth. I saw him. But here's the thing. I saw him twice. He was at one end of the alley, dressed in the way that he was when he left to live in San Francisco. You know. Cholo and junkie style. This wasn't the Todd who dressed like a diamond, who always made sure to look good; he wasn't the bato with whom I would walk through the park and who always made me feel, I don't know, like a queen. No. This was pre-overdose Todd. Skinny, skinny. Sunken eyes. And at the other end of the alley, he was there too. But he wasn't in the cholo look. He was dressed like we used to do when we were kids. You know, normal for the town. In fact, I think he was even wearing a Flash Gordon T-shirt. The first thing I thought was that the loco had become a time traveler for reals and that somehow two versions of him ended up in the same time and place. Freaky, right? I stood up against the alley wall and watched the two of them. And then I knew that I had to make a decision.

I don't answer. I look up at the sky. It's true, I say, one of the things I like most about living in Iowa is that it reminds me of the Orland of our childhood. So much sky. So many open fields. So many stars.

Lupe looks up. Why didn't you call me that night when I was on the hill? I was waiting for you and I knew when you got there. But you never said anything, she tells me.

I don't know what to say. To our right I hear laughter coming from the Sutliff Tavern. There are some children running around in the dark. I look at the cars parked by the river.

Lupe begins to talk. Do you remember when the three of us would play in the tunnels? Remember those games when Todd would make us pretend that we were time travelers or lost astronauts? Todd always loved to look at the stars. Even when we were most out of our minds. He would look up and say random shit, the universe is watching us, or something like that. He also never stopped thinking that he was some kind of lost astronaut. Missing. That's how he saw himself. And you and me, our job was to find him.

It still is, I say.

Snapshots of People I've Known

THIS BEGAN SOMEWHERE BETWEEN Eskişehir and Izmit. Somewhere just past the mountains, out on the flat fields with the afternoon sun hanging low. The train rounded a bend and there they were, a family of goat herders out on the field. A child waved at the passing train. My camera was in my bag at my feet. Not enough time to snap a pic. I stared out the window at the child waving from the field, a thin arm raised into the sky. Then the train flew past and I watched as the child grew smaller and smaller. I returned to looking straight ahead at the back of the blue cloth–covered seat with the Turkish Railways logo neatly printed in red.

———

Eric stands with his back slightly turned to the camera—his face in profile against the night—on the deck of the ferry from Kadıköy to Eminönü. Another ferry passes in the background, its lights blending with those from the Asian shore of Istanbul. He looks out over the water, his hands in his coat pockets, buttoned up against the November chill. Eric was a photographer from Peru living in Istanbul. He told me he wanted to leave the chaos of Lima to experience someplace else. At first, he lived in London, but he missed the locura of what he called ex-centric cities. He moved to Istanbul and found a job with a small advertising agency. We met over in Haydarpaşa Station. I was hungry after the long trip from Ankara so I headed straight for the restaurant. The waiter directed me to a table near the door that opened out onto the waterfront. Eric was at the table next to mine drinking a beer. When he saw me pull out a copy of Josefina Vicens's *El libro vacío*, he started talking to me in Spanish. He soon joined me at my table. I was really not in the mood to talk much as I was tired from the trip. Later, on the ferry to the other shore, I snapped the photo of him looking out over the water.

———

Adela came up to me one night in a bar in Mexico City. I hadn't seen her since we were chiquillos running around the olive orchards in that Northern California town where we grew up. On those nights when our families would take us to the fiestas at the local farms, the kids would break up into groups depending on their age. There were the six-to-nines, the ten-to-thirteens, and then the big kids. The under-sixes were forced to stay close to their parents, who were afraid of losing their children in the orchards. And after five-year-old Alma drowned in one of the irrigation ditches, the parents were even more careful. The ten-to-thirteens had it the worst, we thought. We had to take care of the six-to-nines, and those of us who were close to thirteen wanted to run off with the big kids.

Adela was on the cusp of thirteen while I was still stuck at twelve going on eight. I was far more awkward than her and preferred to sit around talking about comic books with my crew, Fernando and Sam, both eleven, and Lupe, also twelve. We didn't know it then, though we sure sensed it, but our friendship came about because we were the Lost, los Perdidos: terribly awkward, borderline idiots—Sam was the kid who ate paste, picked his nose, and generally liked to burn things; Fernando was mostly mute; and Lupe was also mostly quiet and kept her long straight hair in her face as if she were trying to hide. We were the kids everyone else liked to keep at a distance. Even our parents were close to giving up on us. Moms in particular was busy focusing all her attention on my older brother Todd, who she thought was going to pull us all out of the Sarlac pit where Dad had thrown us after he left.

Occasionally "Toro" Fernández—the only redheaded Mexican I knew at the time—who was my age but acted as if he were fourteen, would come over to give us shit. His favorite was to claim that Green Lantern—one of my favorite superheroes—was actually a border-patrol agent. Look at the green! He would argue before confessing that he thought this was cool. He liked Green Lantern because as an agent of la migra, he too would keep dirty Mexicans in Mexico. When I would complain to my moms, she would just say, Ay m'ijo, why do you let that vendido get to you? His family was closely allied with the growers and so they had a certain power over the other Mexicanos who lived in the area. That privilege was concentrated in Toro—his nickname due to both his temper and his red hair—who used it to lord over us all the way through high school. Last I heard, he became a border-patrol agent.

Adela sometimes joined us in our circle. She had long, straight, jet-black hair just like Lupe, but she would keep it out of her face. Sometimes when we walked home together from school, I would pass her whatever comic I was reading. Her favorite was Batman. The summer she turned fourteen, Adela was increasingly drawn to the older kids. In particular, the cholas: the girls who were fifteen and above; the ones who wore makeup, eyes outlined in thick black eyeliner, who combed their hair high and held it in place with cans of hair spray; the ones who wore baggy pants and tank tops with spaghetti straps; the ones who had nicknames like Sad Girl, Smiley, Hopey, and Maga. I could understand her attraction; the call of the chola was the siren song in the orchards. She moved closer and closer to them, and I was often left to walk home alone.

Within the year, Adela became Giggles, and a couple of years later she began to go out with Ray from Hamilton, the even smaller farming town near ours. He would cruise the ten miles from Hamilton in his lowrider, listening to oldies and whatever barrio music tapes one of his primos from Pacoima sent. When there was a rodeo or a charreada in town, however, Ray would pull out his cowboy clothes. There he would be, at the Freddy Fender concert in his botas, jeans, hat, and shirt with the pearl buttons. Giggles by his side, in her chola wear.

Years later, Adela sees me in a bar in Mexico City. I almost didn't recognize her. Her hair was cut short short and accentuated her thin face; she looked like a Chicana Mia Farrow. She had become a chemical engineer and was living in Mexico City for a few months while conducting a study. We hadn't seen each other in about twenty years, since high school when I left for college and she had been forced by her parents to get a job and forget about studying. We sat at the bar talking about the fiestas at the farms; about how we used to run around in the dark orchards playing hide-and-seek; about how though she was happy to get out of that small farming community, she still often returned to visit with the viejitos, the older generation, and to see how the town was changing. Since my family moved away from there, I had never returned. Later, walking out toward the taxi stand, I take her picture under a streetlamp. She grins broadly and before I take the snap she lifts up her shirtsleeve to show me her tattoo: the Batman logo.

In this photo, Tania looks down at the floor. A cup of coffee in front of her. She is about to tell me something. Muddy Waters Coffee House. San Francisco. Evening. She left her Lebanese-Spanish family in Madrid for San Francisco. It took her four years to arrive. One afternoon, she told her family she was leaving the country and walked out. We met in Schiphol Airport. We were both getting off a flight from Paris. Standing on the moveable walkway heading toward the departure hall, we struck up a conversation about airports. Her favorites were Schiphol, Narita, Munich, and, oddly, Mexico City. This last was on her list because she loved the city. She especially loved flying into it at night when the valley of Mexico was lit up and appeared to be a reflection of the stars above. Her least favorites were JFK, Caracas (Worst. Duty Free. Ever), Heathrow, and Charles de Gaulle. As we had just arrived from that airport, it was singled out for its poor layout and the long distances one had to walk to get to the gate. I agreed and noted that my main gripe with CDG was landing there. It seemed like the runways were on the other side of Paris and the jet had to taxi all around the city before arriving near the terminal, where buses waited to shuttle the passengers for another twenty minutes. We stopped at one of the bars in the departure lounge. While she ate an apple and I drank coffee, she talked about her travels. From Madrid she had gone to London then to Berlin—with a side trip to Kazakhstan where she was an au pair for a summer—then Rio de Janeiro, and, finally, Paris. She was on her way to New York where she had another job lined up. Her hope was to make it to San Francisco. And later, as we walked to our gates, we stopped at one of the glass windows and looked out at the parked jets and tried to guess where they were going. After a while, she looked at me, smiled, and walked away. Two years later we see each other in San Francisco, where I take her picture.

———

Silvio worked the bar at Rosendo's, a hole-in-the-wall antro in

Cholula. A Dominican who left Santo Domingo for New York, he ended up traveling west to Denver, where he hooked up with a collective of young nomads—his description—and ended up crossing the border in El Paso and then continued south past Mexico City to Puebla. The Dominican drifter, I called him. I was living in a friend's apartment in Cholula for the summer. Walking around close to the campus of the Universidad de las Américas, I found Rosendo's bar. It was packed with undergrads from Texas. Study-abroad students, Silvio told me later. They were the bar's best customers as they often headed there for lunch. Rosendo's made some of the best tacos in the area. One would never have guessed with the grimy exterior and rundown look of the place: a perfect description of an antro. In the evenings the place was packed, as the students would return to drink cheap beer and talk loudly about their classes. The bar often contracted a mariachi for parties for the students.

One party Friday, Silvio and I went for a walk around Cholula. He had the day off until the evening, when he had to work the bar. We had lunch in the main plaza of the town and talked over big bowls of sopa azteca. His parents had held high expectations for him—his older brother was a doctor, his younger brother was planning to study law and become a lawyer. As the middle child, he chose to drift. When he showed me a photo of why, I understood. He was on the beach, with his arm around another man who was kissing him on the cheek. A simple gesture, but the look on Silvio's face gave everything away. Rather than come out to their families, his novio became a border guard and moved to Dajabón. Silvio was left with his broken heart and a city that alienated him. He left the island for New York and then kept moving. I know a thing about loss, I told him as we sat outside Rosendo's drinking Tecate. Later, with a mariachi behind him and two students by his side, Silvio smiles for the camera.

———

Lauren was a barista at the Java House in Iowa City. She was from a small town in Iowa and studying at the university. I first met her when I was having my bouts of insomnia. After two weeks of not sleeping for more than an hour, my dream life began to invade my waking life. I felt like I was in a constant state of jet lag. Senses were heightened. Colors more intense. I went one afternoon to buy a cup of coffee and Lauren was at the bar, reading a magazine. I asked for a cup of the St. Louis Blues—a name that resonated with me and was how I always imagined St. Louis, somehow blue because it was tethered to the Mississippi and anchored to the continent as a gateway to the West—and a strawberry danish. It was the last one. She made a joke about how I was now leaving her with no lunch. She explained that she had just started a new diet, the pastry diet. In subsequent visits, I would ask her how the diet was going. Well, she would respond with a smile, I'm losing weight.

I saw her one night with her friends at the Airliner bar. She wore a red dress, accentuating her pale pale skin and dark-blonde hair. All the women around her were in little black dresses, as if cut out from the same mold: cookie-cutter women doing the bar crawl. She recognized me sitting at the bar, drinking a beer and trying to figure out how to sleep. She came over to talk and we ended up leaving the bar together. It was raining and there was thunder and lightning: the whole spectacle of late summer in Iowa. All we needed were the tornado warning sirens going off to complete the scene. We drove an hour across the electrically charged plains to Iowa 80, a place that billed itself as The World's Largest Truck Stop. When she excitedly accepted the offer for coffee at the truck stop I knew that she was going to break my heart. It was then that my insomnia broke and I knew that I was going to be able to sleep again.

She came closest in covering up the absence that my ex-wife, Aidé, had left. Six months after that night at the truck stop, when I felt the urge to pack up and go, she tried to hold me back. At the same time, she knew it was impossible. Movement was the only thing I knew. In her photo, she smiles at me from the cab of a long-haul truck on display in the showroom at Iowa 80. When we were driving back to Iowa City after coffee and pie, I knew that she had inserted a part of herself into me and that as soon as I dropped her off I should start moving again. With haste.

I didn't.

She moved across the city to a soundtrack of mambo, danzón, boleros, and salsa. Pérez Prado. Toña la Negra. Hector Lavoe. Everyone has to have a soundtrack, she told me. One night, under the clichéd blanket of stars, we sat on the old Sutliff Bridge drinking bottled beer and speaking in hushed whispers, as if to not interrupt the sounds of the Cedar River passing below, the crickets, the frogs, and the stars. And months later, when I looked at her photo, I would wonder how she was doing, whether she was still at the Java House reading magazines between customers, walking home from downtown, making random lists in her notebook. Whether she ever thought of me. And after I left, I carried her photo along with the receipt for the coffee and the danish from my first visit to the café in the box where I keep my snapshots.

Years later, when I returned to teach in Iowa City, she was long gone.

———

Roberto stands with the pool cue in his right hand. A pool table between us. His face illuminated by the flash from my camera. He was a geographer at Penn State whom I met one cold winter night standing on a street corner waiting for the light to change. He was a Chilean born in Santiago but raised in Northern California, in Fairfield. Over beer one night, he tells me his perfect '80s moment. It was at the Mabuhay Gardens, the club over in North Beach, in San Francisco, that used to showcase punk shows before closing down in 1986. In 1985 he went with a friend of his to catch X-Mal Deutschland at the Mab. His friend wore a doctor's smock with mysterious stains on it and latex gloves. His hair was spiked with gelatin. Roberto wore torn jeans and a T-shirt for the Zeros, the Chicano punk band from L.A. During the warm-up, where a couple of transvestites in lingerie lip synced to German torch songs, he made his way through the crowd to the front of the stage. Before the house lights went down he noticed the most beautiful woman he'd ever seen. A punk rock pachuca princess, he declares, pool cue in hand, lining up a shot. Her hair was spiked Siouxsie Sioux style, her eyes outlined in heavy black eyeliner, her lips painted black. She wore a torn, thin white T-shirt and a black bra underneath, a tartan miniskirt over torn fishnets, black patent leather boots, and a look of utter boredom on her face. Roberto looked at her beside him and the lights went out. When they came back on, Anja Huwe, the lead singer of X-Mal Deutschland, was standing over him on stage. The band started into "Mondlicht." While everyone in the club began to jump around, the punk rock barrio princess and Roberto remained still, locked in place looking up at the band.

At one point, they looked at each other. And everything froze: the club, the crowd, the band, the music. Only the two remained, Roberto and the barrio princess looking at one another illuminated by the bright stage lights. It seemed like a long moment, the two of them looking at each other.

Then everything started up again.

The band was performing "Boomerang," the crowd was leaping all around; the barrio princess returned to her gaze of detachment. That was it. His perfect '80s moment. At three in the morning, after the show was over, Roberto and his friend ended up at the IHOP in Berkeley. The crowd from the showing of *The Rocky Horror Picture Show* at the Berkeley theater had also arrived, mixing with the punks from the Mab who lived in the East Bay. The two crowds mixed effortlessly, though at any other time or place they might have called out insults to each other. He never saw the barrio princess again.

Mariya was from Ukraine and was a travel writer. She was trying to convince me to be her new travel buddy. She began by talking about her former partner, Antonia. They met in college, and together they had traveled through Latin America and Asia. Camping on the beach in Puerto Escondido; bus trips through the Himalayas; walking around the Incan walled streets of Ollantaytambo; a week in an old hotel in Phnom Penh while working as crew for a documentary on Cambodia. After a few years, Antonia had gone off to live in Turkmenistan and Mariya was in need of a new travel partner. Everyone needs one, she told me. We were sitting in Luis's apartment in Playas de Tijuana. The sliding glass door was open and we could hear the waves outside. Luis had left us the place for a few days while he had gone on some mysterious trip to Veracruz. Mariya leaned back in her chair, her shoulder-length red hair against the wall, in her hand a bottle of Tecate. I had arrived in Tijuana looking for Luis but found Mariya instead. He left a note telling me not to worry about her. Just another friend who arrived a few days before me. She was staying in the guest room and I got the futon in the study. Two nights later, I was also in the guest room. Sitting in the living room with the sounds of the ocean outside, she talked about having pizza in Cali, Colombia, with students from the university. Of the walks around the city she took with them—every place where they stopped had a story about a kidnapping, or an escape, or a shootout. And yet, she told me, no one seemed afraid. One night they all went to a local disco where they spent hours dancing salsa and drinking rum. The whole city seemed abuzz with movement, with excitement at the same time that there seemed to be an undercurrent of imminent danger. I take her photo standing on the balcony. Her hair blowing in the wind, her lips curled into a sly grin. She's wearing one of my T-shirts that she would later keep. We separated a few days later. She was off to

Chiapas and I was on a bus bound for Cabo San Lucas. She wanted us to meet again in Palenque, but I only made it as far as Mexico City before boarding a flight for Lima.

———

Bozan drove a taxi in Madrid. One night after drinking in a bar in Lavapies with friends, I walked down to the plaza to find a taxi to take me to the airport. The rule we had in Spain was that if we had a flight that left before noon, we had to stay out all night. At four I found a taxi to take me to Cuatro Caminos, where I had been staying, to pick up my bag. From there, we went to Barajas. Bozan was Kurdish, from Tatvan on Lake Van. Driving out to the airport we talked about migration and its consequences. About insatiable longings for elsewheres. In the background we listened to a compilation of Kurdish music. Songs, I gathered, about migration and wandering. Due to the difficulties of finding a job in Turkey, Bozan had ended up working in Germany, then Italy, and finally Spain. He was far from home but he found connection in other ways: in telephone calls, in e-mail messages, in conversations with other immigrant friends in Lavapies. He was a part of a larger migrant community, homeless in many ways. Over the stereo Aynur sang of wandering while Bozan told me his story. I remembered Aidé and her complaints about my travels, of the people I've known and their forms of departure. I thought of Lauren and her questions on why I felt the need to constantly move. When he dropped me off I asked if I could take his photo. He stands stiffly beside the white taxi, a thin smile on his face. As I'm about to walk away he stops me, heads back into his taxi, and hands me the CD he had been playing.

A gift, he says.

———

It all started on the train from Ankara to Istanbul. This taking of snapshots of people I've known. There are, of course, some that I don't have. I don't carry any photos of Aidé, for example. Sometimes I wish I did. Most times I just have the memory. Aidé on our wedding day, lying back on the bed of our hotel room with her dress unbuttoned and eating chocolate chip cookies. Aidé with her feet in the air, reading a book in our cramped apartment, a look of concentration on her face, a pencil in one hand. Aidé waiting for me at the airport when I arrived from another trip, her face bursting into a smile and her arms opening wide to embrace me. Aidé crying over dinner as we try to avoid the issue of a marriage that was reaching its end. Aidé walking out the door for the last time, and me later placing the remnants of our house in boxes, packing a bag of clothes, and then walking out for a trip that had no end.

La línea

THE BORDER AGENT LOOKS at you, but you can only see yourself reflected in his mirrored sunglasses. You are sitting behind the wheel of the old white Mustang. The agent is interrogating you. Asking you the typical questions; you already know them all. But you have to act as if it is the first time you have heard them and take them as seriously as if you were interviewing for a job. A job where you would have to risk your life with the incessant traffic of Southern California; the migra checkpoints; the helicopters—from the television networks, the highway patrol, the armed forces, and the border patrol—flying over the landscape; and all the other daily difficulties that make living in these borderlands so different. Never a dull moment. Nonstop excitement. This is what the border interview promises you. Another side that is like this side but only with a different government but a similar attitude of disdain for its border communities.

The questions:

What was your purpose for your visit to Mexico?

What are you bringing from Mexico?

Sometimes there are others: Where were you born, where are you going, who owns this car? If the agent wants, they can ask you the same question up to five times.

You think that it might have been better if you had stayed in Tijuana, sitting on a terraza looking out over the sea, a line of beer—Tecate, Pacífico, Sol, whatever was served—waiting for you while you watched the sun dip into the ocean. And later, you would cross the street to shoot pool with the usual gang, drinking Tecate and listening to '80s music from the jukebox.

But no. There you are. On the line. La línea.

While the agent asks you the usual questions, you want to respond:

To lose myself a while.

Nothing. Nothing more than my dead.

Nothing more than a notebook full of stories, and a camera filled with snapshots of people.

But how could the border-patrol agents understand, they who have never truly felt what it means to wander? How could they understand a trip stitched together by stories and photographs?

Where am I going?

¿A dónde voy?

Home. A mi home.

But at that precise moment, you really don't know where it is. You see yourself reflected in the agent's sunglasses. He is interrogating you so that you can be allowed back into your country. And at that moment, you realize that you would much rather stay there, in that space between nations. Stuck in that moment, without going forward or backward. To think about what you were going to do. Where you were going.